A SINISTER STATUE,
A STRANGE RELIGION ...

No one particularly liked the new statue in Johnny Redfield's rose garden. It had the look of something that had once been alive. Had his sun-worshiping aunt installed it in honor of Apollo? Or did it conceal a more sinister secret?

When the wealthy widow was suddenly shot, Henry Gamadge discovered that nothing was what it seemed to be at the idyllic country estate ... that beneath the polite conversation lay a motive for murder and behind the friendly smiles lay the smoldering hatred of a dangerous killer.

... AND SUDDEN DEATH
IN THE AFTERNOON.

Murder Ink.® Mysteries

Scene Of The Crime™ Mysteries

A Murder Ink.®Mystery

ANY SHAPE
OR FORM

Elizabeth Daly

A DELL BOOK

Published by
Dell Publishing Co., Inc.
1 Dag Hammarskjold Plaza
New York, New York 10017

Dell ® TM 681510, Dell Publishing Co., Inc.

ISBN: 0-440-10108-5

Reprinted by arrangement with Holt, Rinehart and
Winston, CBS Educational & Professional Publishing,
a division of CBS, Inc.

Printed in the United States of America

First Dell printing—September 1981

1

Something in a Garden

"Look through here, Henry," said Miss Ryder. "You can see it if you look through here."

Gamadge, pretending interest—Miss Abigail Ryder was his only female relative and seventy years old—peered through the meshes of the seven-foot wire fence into greenery. He said: "I can't see a thing."

Miss Ryder took hold of his arm and jerked him closer to her side: "Look where I'm looking."

Gamadge could do so only by further reducing his own height. He bent, flattened his nose against the wire, and gazed earnestly through the gap in the inner hedge. He could now see across a broad lawn, through a trellised archway, and to the very end of an enclosed garden. After a moment he asked incredulously: "What on earth?"

Miss Ryder said triumphantly: "You tell me!"

"Can't tell you. Never saw anything like it."

"Whatever it is, imagine Johnny Redfield putting it up in his rose garden!"

"Must be a curio. But even if it is, where's his celebrated taste we never hear the end of?"

"You're such a detective," said Miss Ryder in a bantering tone; she was of the old school, and thought that younger generations ought to be kept in their place. "You're such a detective, I supposed you'd give one look at it and tell me exactly what it was."

"In five minutes we can ask Redfield what it is. I don't know why you haven't asked him before."

"I haven't seen him all summer—not since I caught my first glimpse of that horror on my way up to the other cocktail party; the one he gave for his aunt when she first came. And there was such a crowd at the house that it went out of my mind."

"When was that?"

"The second Sunday in July. Mrs. Malcolm came at the end of June, I think."

"You haven't seen Johnny Redfield since July? I thought you were always dropping in on each other."

"We haven't the use of our cars now, and this hill is getting to be too much for me in warm weather, and Johnny never puts foot to the ground if he can help it. And I've been away myself most of the summer; only got back to the cottage the first of September."

"Well, you're doing your duty today." Gamadge removed his nose from the wire and dusted it off with his handkerchief. "You not only came, you dragged me. I don't particularly wish to meet Redfield's aunt from California."

"He'll be so pleased to see you. And it's her farewell party, she's going next week. And it's a great occasion besides."

"What great occasion?"

But his cousin was again peering through the gap in the hedge. She said: "Johnny always meant to have a fountain there at the end of the middle path; he thought of putting it in when he put in the other

ANY SHAPE OR FORM 7

waterworks—the cascades and pools in the rockery. Just the place for a fountain; pipes came down from a spring in the woods and fed the old watering trough. It was where the rose garden is now, as I remember it, and the barns and carriage house where this lawn is, and the cow barns down below; the duck pond was turned into the swimming pool. The lawn and all the big maples were in front of the house—I loved the old Redfield place. I was here a great deal, when Johnny's parents were alive and he was in his gocart."

"Why didn't he put a fountain in?"

"He wanted to pick one up in Europe."

"But never found one he could comfortably carry?"

"He picked up a handsome iron urn and put it there. Why on earth should he have taken it away and put up that repulsive object? It wasn't there last summer. I never saw it until that day in July when I was walking up and noticed that a tree was gone from the hedge—I suppose it died in the cold spell last winter. Johnny probably couldn't get it replaced—you saw the condition *my* shrubbery's in! I stopped, and saw that I could look through; and there, among all the roses, stood that thing. And before I got over the shock a tree spoke to me."

Gamadge looked down at her. "Are you getting whimsical at last, Cousin Ab?"

"It's those parrots. They're loose in the grounds all summer, and one of them was in that little mountain ash there. It gabbled something and laughed. I didn't wait to hear what it was trying to say, I can tell you! I made off up the hill."

"I don't think you were much disturbed," said Gamadge, "except by the looks of Johnny's new antique.

It would take more than a battered image and a
disembodied voice to bother you."

"But what can the thing be, Henry?"

Gamadge bent to peer again. "Well, it's pretty far
off; but I can see that it represents a human figure,
probably masculine, and less than life size. There's a
suggestion of short classical drapery. The figure is
mounted on a low, rounded base, and it's badly
weathered and defaced."

"Defaced? Mutilated! It *has* no face! And look at
those stumps of hands out in front of it—clutching!"

"They're not clutching; they were holding something. Some emblem—a musical instrument or a cor-
nucopia."

"A wooden thing will simply rot away. If Johnny
had to put up something ugly, he might have put up
that hideous stone toad he brought back from Indo-
China."

"Wood," said Gamadge. "Funny. One doesn't see
garden gods and statuary made of wood. But a saint,
now—an early Christian saint without its shrine? Con-
vert from a Roman legion? It's wearing a short tunic,
and I think high buskins. May have been painted or
gilt. Or how about one of the more militant angels—
wings gone, but something that might be the remains
of a halo is sticking out of the head. Or a scriptural
character? I've seen big wooden figures—Spanish—
from those Christmas groups. What do you call
them?"

Miss Ryder, tiring of these ruminations, jerked Gamadge's arm. She said: "You don't know any more
about it than I do. Come along. Johnny said four
o'clock."

Gamadge obediently turned, and walked at her side

along the grass border of the private lane. But he protested: "People always want me to guess at things, but they always get tired of the subject before I stop guessing."

His cousin snatched at her hat as the wind caught it, and crammed it back on her head. She complained: "You *plod* so."

Gamadge, adapting his pace to hers, strolled beside her with his hands in his pockets. He was hatless and in tweeds, his head lifted gratefully to the gentle October breeze. His amiable features looked happy. He was seldom grave; one Macloud, a saturnine friend, had in fact been known under stress to ask him to take his grinning face out of there. But not even Macloud had ever found his laughter causeless or malign.

Looking now across the road, beyond the fence and hedge that bounded the higher property on the other side of the way, he asked idly how the Drummonds were.

Miss Ryder answered in a tone of restraint that they were quite well, so far as she knew, and that they would be at the party that afternoon.

Gamadge looked at her. "Anything more than usually wrong with them?"

"I don't know what you mean," said Miss Ryder, who was sternly opposed to gossip.

"Well, I mean that I've never seen Blanche and Walter exchange a word or a look in the last five years."

"You only see them at parties. In case you didn't know it, married persons are not supposed to talk privately in public, or stare at each other."

"I stare at Clara a good deal. Come on, Abby; tell me: has Blanche worn him out at last?"

"Worn him out! Walter was always *devoted—*"

"She'd wear me out in three days; beautiful as she is. I suppose I could last three days—looking at her."

"If he didn't care for the type, he needn't have married her."

"People like Walter Drummond always think the statue will some day come to life. But I should think the time would come when even Pygmalion would up with the mallet."

"Walter Drummond," said Miss Ryder, frowning, "isn't the kind to up with a mallet. I suppose you mean lose patience and go?"

"Lose patience and go—or something." He strolled on, whistling softly; but glancing down at his cousin, and seeing that her cheerful face looked worried, he fished about for a change of subject.

"You said this party of Johnny Redfield's was a great occasion. Is he celebrating because he's getting rid of Aunt after having her with him from the second Sunday in July until the middle of October?"

"Johnny must be rather tired of entertaining her, I should think. She's very odd."

"Is she?"

"Very. Johnny told me he was a little anxious about her making the trip back to California alone, she's so flighty now. He says she turned her companion off before she came, and is sick of them, and won't have another. I should think she's developed the flightiness since she's been a widow, though, because Johnny told me Mr. Archibald Malcolm was a most hardheaded, conventional old thing. He was from one of those Scotch-pioneer Canadian families;

but he'd settled in America—in the Northwest—for a long time; was making money in lumber. He's been dead ten years; she's been living in Pasadena."

"Plenty of time and opportunity to get flighty," said Gamadge. "Did you know her here in the old days?"

"No, she wasn't here much; liked travel. It was in Europe that she met the Archibald Malcolms, some years before the first Mrs. Malcolm died. Johnny's aunt was quite middle-aged when she married the widower; she must be at least sixty now. She's never been East since she married, and she adores Pasadena. But Johnny managed to get her back at last."

"How did he manage it?"

"She's meeting her stepchildren here today for the first time—David and Cora Malcolm."

"Really! Why hasn't she met them before?"

"Because they wouldn't have anything to do with her. Their mother was ill for years before she died—tuberculosis—and in a Swiss sanitarium. They were put in Swiss schools when they were only seven or eight, to be near her. The father doesn't seem to have bothered much about them or about her, I must say. He was making money in Oregon, or wherever it was, and never went abroad to see them. Then she died, and he married Miss Josephine Redfield within the year. A very successful marriage, Johnny says, but he didn't live long to enjoy it. The children were about thirteen, then at the time of the marriage, I mean—and they were so disagreeable about it that he allowed them to stay over there; in fact, they wouldn't come home. They've been there ever since until the war—first in Switzerland and then in schools in England, and after their father died they settled in

France. Now they live together in an apartment in New York. Did I say they were twins?"

"No. They sound like young persons of determination."

"People have never blamed them much for their attitude, though they've never blamed Johnny's Aunt Josephine either. And then this wretched old Archibald Malcolm died and left the children only small allowances, and all the rest of his money to their stepmother for life."

"Whew. That *was* getting even with the offspring!"

"Well, yes; but I suppose he was furious because they were so disagreeable about his second marriage."

"Perhaps they'd got some idea from their mother, or injudicious friends, that Johnny's Aunt Josephine had worked on old Mr. Malcolm in advance—before the first wife died."

"I never heard that anybody ever said that."

"How much does the stepmother get per annum?"

"About fifty thousand, I believe."

"And what happens when she dies?"

"Then it goes to the twins, share and share alike."

"And she wants to meet them?" Gamadge pretended horror.

"Very much. She's always wanted to be friends with them. She's offered them twice what they get now. They've always refused, but this summer they agreed to take it."

"And what's softened their hearts at last?"

"Johnny. You know Johnny; he does so hate it when people don't get on. The first Mrs. Malcolm liked him, and so did the children; he'd met the whole family in Europe through his aunt, and then—wasn't it just like him?—he used to go and see the first

wife in her sanitarium whenever he was abroad—
which as you know was every spring—and he used to
go and see the children in their schools. They never
blamed *him;* he felt awfully about the will. Since
they've been in this country he's seen a lot of them,
and had them up here in the summers. He's worked
on their sense of justice."

"To themselves?" Gamadge was amused. He asked:
"Do the young Malcolms perhaps find living expenses
higher in this country than in France before the
war?"

"If that has something to do with their making
friends with the stepmother," said Miss Ryder, "I
shan't blame them at all. But Johnny says he's convinced them that his Aunt Josephine didn't influence
old Mr. Malcolm when he made that will. He says she
was dumbfounded."

"Does she look like a good insurance risk, Abby?"

"Oh mercy, yes; she's wiry."

"Her stepchildren will be middle-aged before they
get their father's money. Very tough. What branch of
the services," asked Gamadge, "is young Malcolm in?"

"No branch. He was injured in France in nine-
teen-forty."

"Fighting for his adopted country?"

"No; getting away."

"Have you met the twins?"

"Several times. They've often been here in the summers since they came back."

"What are they like?"

"Judge for yourself this afternoon. I can't quite
make them out, myself. They're very clever and
good-looking, but somehow—I don't quite know
why—I always get the impression that they never

mean what they say. They never seem serious; and without being ill-bred about it, they always seem to have some private joke with each other. Johnny says it's being twins; I don't know." Miss Ryder rubbed her left ear. "I should think he'd be very nervous about the meeting this afternoon. I simply can't imagine them getting on with Mrs. Malcolm. She'd stun them."

"Sensitive, are they? What do they do?"

"Do?"

"What have they been doing with themselves besides hating their stepmother?"

"I think they write."

"Publish?"

"I don't suppose so, or Johnny would have said something. He thinks they're wonderful. The boy made a very unfortunate marriage in France. Johnny says they're both changed since they got home."

"And you think they're warped and malicious? Or at least unamiable?"

"I make allowances. Their mother was a sick woman, and I think she was a neglected woman, and they were under her influence for years. And they've been living with rather disillusioned people, I think. They're polite enough, certainly to me, but I imagine that they rather despise us all."

She paused. They had arrived at a fork in the road, where two signs hung from a post by ornamental brackets. The right-hand sign was simply inscribed with the name *Drummond*. The left-hand one said IDLERS. *J. M. Redfield*.

" 'Idlers'!" said Miss Ryder crossly. "Imagine calling the old Redfield place Idlers! The natives pronounced it Iddlers from the first; they never did know what Johnny meant by it."

"He meant what he said," declared Gamadge, "and Idlers is an excellent name for it now. Then it was a farm; now it's a summer place to idle in."

"Johnny thinks it's a great joke, their calling it Iddlers."

"Johnny would."

The left fork of the road wound under huge evergreens; pine needles lay thick on the sandy track, and the sky was no more than a ribbon of blue. Through dense trees on the left there was a glimpse of a house.

Gamadge and Miss Ryder passed a garage and a stone cottage on their right, and came out on a circular driveway; beyond it rose the unbroken line of the woods. The house, once a solid square of pinkish-drab native stone, now elongated by a north and a south wing, fronted the drive.

"Is Redfield painting much nowadays?" asked Gamadge, as they mounted the shallow doorstep. He was glancing to his right, where the studio occupied the whole of the south wing.

"Dabbling," said Miss Ryder.

"Rather nice dabbling. All in black and white still?"

"I suppose so."

"I never see him in New York."

"He moves about so much. Did I tell you that he goes out to Pasadena every spring to see his Aunt Josephine?"

"No."

"He says she lives such a secluded life there; she has a house with walled grounds, and she won't leave the place."

"Sounds rather restful," said Gamadge idly.

"I don't think she'd fit into ordinary society now."

"Poor Redfield."

"He really is fond of her, and quite worried about her now that she's got rid of that Miss Gouch."

"Miss Gouch?"

"The companion. Johnny says Miss Gouch was really an excellent person. Now the aunt will be alone, for a while at least, and Johnny doesn't like it. She's getting very queer, Henry."

The door opened, and a nice-looking young colored girl in a wine-colored uniform and frilled apron smiled at them.

"How do you do, Alice?" asked Miss Ryder. "How's your mother?"

"She's fine, Miss Ryder, thank you. How do you do, Mr. Gamadge?"

"Nice to see you again, Alice."

"Nice to see you, Mr. Gamadge. Please excuse the delay in answering the door."

"Don't tell me you're short-handed," smiled Gamadge.

"Yes, sir, we are. We only have Tilly Wirtz, and now Sam's gone too. Poor Mr. Redfield has to drive himself."

"Oh Lord; poor Redfield."

"Yes, sir. We have some nice little pears for you, Miss Ryder, if Mr. Gamadge will carry the basket down. You know George left for defense in the spring, and now we only have an occasional man in the gardens, and the Wilson boy. Of course they're not here on Sunday. It isn't the way it was when George lived over the garage."

"It was kind of whoever thought of the pears at

all," said Miss Ryder. "Have them ready, and Mr. Gamadge will carry them home for me."

They passed Alice and went into the hall; it extended through to glass doors that opened east on a terrace, and also on a fine view of trees and sky. A delicate stairway rose on the right; it had been salvaged from some other statelier house to take the place of the enclosed flight which had once led up to the second story of the old Redfield farm.

Alice said with an apologetic glance at the empty copper jug on a side table: "We just don't get to do the flowers right any more, Miss Ryder, unless Mr. Redfield finds the time."

"Don't blame you," said Abigail.

"And we don't have as many flowers as we had when George was here. But Mr. Redfield says perhaps some of the folks will pick flowers this afternoon."

"I can't. I have my rheumatism just now."

"So has Mother."

"Give her my sympathy."

A slim man in his middle forties, short, baldish, with a neat moustache and bright hazel eyes, rushed from a doorway beyond the stairs. He seized Miss Ryder's hands. "Abby, I never see you now. Gamadge, my boy, I'm glad Abigail lured you up. But I'm disappointed not to see your wife with you."

"Er," said Gamadge. "She's still on Long Island hanging over the sky-blue bassinet."

"Great heavens, how could I have forgotten?"

"Henry would be doing the same," said Miss Ryder, "if he hadn't had a call of distress from me. I realized that I could never do my December tax installment without him; not to mention the thing that comes in March."

"My God, can he do them? Can anybody? Well, thank goodness you're both here. I'm counting on you. Go in, Abby, do. Things seem to be getting a little sticky in there."

"I thought they might be," said Miss Ryder, and walked past the stairs and on into the living room.

Alice had lingered. She said: "Mr. Redfield, excuse me, but I think we're going to need some more of the Mount Gay."

"Oh—do they like it? Good. Here's the key. You don't mind bringing it up, Alice? Thanks." As she disappeared through an archway on the left, Redfield turned back to Gamadge. "I'm my own butler now, as you see; and I'm my own chauffeur, and getting to be my own gardener. Abby's told you what this occasion is, Gamadge, I suppose?"

"Something."

2

A Token

Redfield was looking anxious. "The children are behaving pretty well," he said. "Pretty well. But poor
dear Aunt Joise—they hardly know how to take her.
You'll help, Gamadge? You'll do your best? You won't
mind humoring her? She'll ask you to call her Vega,
you know; that's her astrological name." He smiled.
"You won't mind a flight to the stars? Into the Inane?
I refer, of course, to the immensities of space." His
eyes glinted. "Just to keep her happy, you know. She's
such a decent old thing."

Gamadge said gravely that she had done well to
choose as a patron a star of the first magnitude.

"Well, she sticks to the name; but I'm afraid that
apart from sticking to the name she's rather deserted
astrology. I'm afraid it's a sun cult now."

"A what?"

"A sun cult."

"I don't know about sun cults," protested Gamadge. "I couldn't talk intelligently about sun cults."

"Gamadge, my boy, you won't be called upon to
talk intelligently about a damned thing. I can't keep
up myself. But after all, it's all in the System, isn't it?
Just humor her, old man."

"Count on me." Gamadge followed him into the living room.

It was a delightful room, long, high and bright, with double windows to the east and west. The front and back parlors of the old Redfield place had been thrown into one, and gaily papered and upholstered with Chinese birds and flowers. The best of the original mantelpieces had been set into the middle of the south wall, and a fire burned on the hearth.

There were six persons in the room, two on the west window seat and four around the fire; Gamadge, pausing in the doorway while Redfield snatched drink and food for him from Alice's tray, glanced at them all. The two at the window were his cousin Abigail and Mrs. Walter Drummond; the group that surrounded the hearth consisted of two young people on a settee, Walter Drummond in front of the fire on their left, and opposite them a figure that looked as though it might be dressed up for a fantastic part in a charade. Blanche Drummond, who if she were listening to Abby could certainly not have been attending to her, turned her head on its long and beautiful neck, smiled at Gamadge, and extended a hand in a long, creamy glove.

"Well, Henry," she said.

"Well, Blanche." He advanced to take the hand. "You're looking splendid. But have you ever looked less than splendid?"

She was thirty-five years old and didn't look it; tall, white-skinned, with bronze-golden hair and eyes the color, and with the brilliance, of the stone called cat's eye. In her woolen suit that had been dyed to simulate the tint of a dead leaf, with the bronze feather of her little hat drooping almost to one of her large gold-and-pearl earrings, she was a lady from the cover of an art-and-fashion magazine; she had such a lady's calm, resigned, distant look.

Blanche Drummond hardly every smiled, yet never looked serious; she looked blank. But was there a troubled expression in her face today, and had she aged a little? Gamadge thought so, and Abby's restraint when speaking of her had half prepared him for something of the kind.

Before she had replied to his compliment Johnny Redfield bustled up and dragged him away. "You mustn't talk to people you know yet, Gamadge; you must come and meet my aunt. Here's your cocktail and here's your sandwich." His voice dropped. "I suggest that you swallow the cocktail *now;* then I'll bring you another."

Gamadge, swallowing his cocktail, glanced again at the group in front of the fire. The two young Malcolms, side by side on their settee, had turned to look at him; and whether it was the identical quick motion of their dark heads, or the quizzical expression in their dark eyes, he couldn't for the life of him help thinking of two very intelligent monkeys. But they were both handsome, and certainly not ill-proportioned. The next moment they were simply an attractive young man and woman in tweeds, with clear olive complexions, low and broad foreheads, short, straight noses, and well-shaped chins. They had brown hands, with strong fingers. The young man, when he rose, showed himself to be medium tall, with wide shoulders. The girl seemed more delicately made.

Next to her, and leaning forward in his chair as if he had been listening or talking to her, sat Walter

Drummond; tall, big and sandy, with a small sandy moustache, and wearing rough country tweeds. On the little table between them Walter's cigarette burned itself away in its glass dish. He looked up over his shoulder at Gamadge, and rose; but his blue eyes hardly seemed to recognize his old acquaintance.

Alone at the other end of the hearth sat the odd figure of the sun worshiper; a woman who would have looked shrewd, even rather hard and sharp, if it had not been for a grotesque costume and a wild and wandering eye. Gamadge had to remind himself that "big" business men consulted palmists, clairvoyants, and astrologers, in order to reconcile that Roman nose, thin mouth, and firm jaw, with the wreath of yellow artificial flowers on Vega's graying hair; with the yellow robe that hardly reached her bare ankles and was tied about her waist with a white cord obviously torn from a dressing gown; with the toeless and heelless beach sandals, yellow and blue, that could scarcely be said to cover her bare feet. There were rings on her fingers, and the left breast of the robe was decorated with a large diamond cluster, old-fashioned in design.

"Vega," said Johnny Redfield, "let me present Henry Gamadge. Abigail Ryder's cousin, you know."

Vega's smile was benevolent, and she held out her hand graciously, even mincingly. The refined gesture went oddly with the stare of the pale eyes and the slightly mad effect of the fillet and the robe. But they, of course, might be ritual—appropriate to somebody's idea of a cult of the sun.

Redfield said: "Gamadge is here by the happiest chance, Aunt. In these difficult times he doesn't look in on us often."

"I'm delighted to meet Miss Ryder's nephew," said Vega. "Or cousin—cousin, of course. Have you met my stepchildren?"

Gamadge said he hadn't as yet had the pleasure.

"Cora, this is Mr. Gamadge, Mr. Gamadge, David Malcolm."

Gamadge exchanged bows with the young Malcolms, and shook hands with Drummond. Chairs were pulled up; Gamadge found himself between the sun worshiper and Redfield. The twins sat quietly, shoulder to shoulder, gazing at Vega with a kind of innocent wonder; but Gamadge had seldom seen two people who looked more alert and wary.

"Did you know that it's our first meeting, Mr. Gamadge?" asked Vega, swinging a sandaled foot. "Our very first! These dear children have been living abroad, you know, or did live abroad until the war drove them home three years ago. And I have been living very quietly in Pasadena; more and more I hate to leave my peaceful, *sun-drenched* home! And when the rains do come, I go to the desert. But it couldn't go on forever, you know—our not coming together. Now it's all going to be different. We shall meet often. If I'm able I shall come East every summer."

"Able?" protested Redfield. "Of course you'll be able."

"I mean if I'm still on earth in this shape," said Vega, smiling brightly at him. "In this vesture of decay, you know."

Cora Malcolm was leaning forward, her hands clasped around her crossed knee, her eyes fixed on the speaker. Her brother's hand was along the back of the settee. He tapped her shoulder lightly, as he said in the low, unaccented monotone that both the twins affected: "I don't quite follow the trend of the idea, Mrs. Malcolm."

"Vega, my dearest boy. Call me Vega."

"I must remember. What I mean is, we should expect to find the old symbols—of fertility, of revival—in any cult of the sun. What dies in the autumn comes up in the spring. But slowly, if surely! Gradually and chemically."

"Or botanically," said Cora.

"Or botanically. But you almost seem to imply, Mrs. Malcolm—excuse me, I can't get used to it yet—that in your case you expect the translation to be immediate, quasi-miraculous. The quite different symbolism of the butterfly and the cocoon."

"I do mean that," said Vega, complacently. Though Redfield moved in his chair, and even Walter Drummond shuffled his feet, she had not seemed to notice that she was being made fun of. "I do mean it," she repeated. "But you mustn't inquire too closely into the mysteries, dear boy. You wouldn't understand."

Redfield said gaily: "Dearest Aunt, I preferred the stars! The stars were confusing enough, but at least seemed to be definite about what was going to happen to us."

"I really prefer Calvin to the stars," said David Malcolm, his dark eyes turning to Redfield. "I'd rather be predestined by Calvin than by the stars."

"But the stars," said Cora, "let us alone after we die. Don't they?"

Vega wore an expression vague but tolerant. Gamadge wondered why she put up with the twins, why they risked losing the increase in their allowance by their recklessness. Or had they gauged, as they thought, her silliness, and decided that open mockery would be safe? Looking again at that cold, canny face, he was more than ever certain that its owner was credulous—even perhaps a little crazy—on one subject and one alone. Like those big business men.

And he reflected that there might be something to account for her patience with the twins, something more rational than a bewitched preoccupation with the mysteries of a sun cult. Vega might be suffering from a guilty conscience where the young Malcolms were concerned. She really might have influenced her husband against them when he made his will. She might have read something in the stars—or the sun— which told her to make amends. In that case she wouldn't allow her stepchildren's rudeness to dissuade her from giving them money.

He remarked, in the tone of one who brings matters to a plane where everybody must feel at home: "I never did think that Casca was entirely right when he snubbed Brutus about the stars."

"And who, pray," asked Vega, smilingly, "was Casca?"

"Pay no attention to him," said Redfield, "or to David either. They're both showing off. Why not? David is a prodigy who hasn't had a chance to express himself creatively yet; and as for Gamadge, what can you expect of an intelligence so perverse that its owner can only refer to his son and heir as a sky-blue bassinet?"

David Malcolm, with a faint indication of distaste for this domestic reminder, said that it surely couldn't be showing off on Mr. Gamadge's part to allude to anything so obvious as *Julius Caesar*.

"I owe you one," said Gamadge, smiling at him.

"But Casca isn't obvious to me," declared Vega.

"Just a friend of dear Brutus'," Malcolm told her, "informing him that man is master of his fate."

"I hate to seem pedantic," said Gamadge, "but I must point out that Casca qualified his statement. He only said that men are at *some time* masters of their fate."

David Malcolm grinned. "Now we're even," he said.

"Er—not quite."

Vega looked bewildered.

Miss Ryder and Mrs. Drummond approached the circle, chairs were rearranged. Abigail addressed Redfield accusingly:

"Johnny, you've lost a tree out of your boundary hedge."

"Don't remind me, Abby! It went in February. Some blight."

"Did you know," she continued, and the oblique approach to her subject amused Gamadge very much, "that people can see right across the lawn and right into your rose garden?"

"Can they? I didn't realize that the gap was in a straight line from the archway. And why should I mind their seeing in?"

"No reason why, if you don't mind giving them a shock."

"Shock?"

"Johnny, what *is* that horrid wooden image you've put up there?"

"Oh!" Redfield glanced at Vega, who looked complacent. "You had a glimpse of our little monster, had you?"

"Let's make them guess what it is," said Vega, swinging her foot until the sandal hung from one toe. "And guess where it came from."

"I guess that it once held something in its hands," said Gamadge.

"It held a lyre, Mr. Gamadge!" Vega was delighted with him. "At least Johnny and I are sure it held a lyre. Now there's a clue for you!"

"Wait a minute." Gamadge smiled at her. "Did *you* make Johnny put the thing up?"

"Of course I did."

"And your favorite star is now our own star—the sun. Is it a figure of Apollo?"

"Of course! Didn't you see the rays on his head?"

"Well, I never saw a wooden image of Apollo before in all my life."

"And why," asked David Malcolm in his tired monotone, "why Apollo in a rose garden?"

"Apollo Smintheus," said Gamadge. "And by the look on your face, Mr. Malcolm, I think that now we *are* even."

"We are. I don't know Apollo in that rôle, whatever it may be."

"Destroyer of field mice." Gamadge turned to accept another cocktail from Alice, and another canapé.

Vega clapped her hands. "Johnny!" she exclaimed, and gave a little screech of delight. "Do you hear? Our Apollo protects the garden!"

"Splendid," said Johnny.

"Do anything about Japanese beetles?" mumbled Walter Drummond. "If so, might lend him to us."

"I wouldn't let Johnny lend him to anybody," cried Vega.

"We need him here," agreed Johnny. "Especially if

he does do anything about Japanese beetles. Does he, Gamadge?"

"Not that I know of," replied Gamadge. "Field mice, just field mice."

David Malcolm showed amusement. He turned to his sister. "This really seems to be a nice man, Cora," he said. "A very nice man."

Johnny burst out laughing. "Ever so nice, Dave," he chuckled. "And the soul of urbanity, too—unless he's crossed. When he's crossed, he's poison."

"Well, really!" said Miss Ryder. "I don't flatter people. I *never* flatter my own relations; but I must say that a more foolishly good-natured creature than Henry Gamadge I don't believe exists on earth."

"Thank you, Abby," said Gamadge, in a meek voice.

"I agree with you, Abigail; we find him so," said Johnny. But then we haven't committed any crimes."

"I thought Mr. Gamadge liked crimes," said Malcolm, in a tone of faint surprise.

Cora said: "We thought he took only an academic interest in them. Oh dear. Does he live to avenge them? Then he can't be so nice after all."

"Once in a while a crime hits me the wrong way," said Gamadge diffidently. "I've had a little luck with some of those."

"And we never knew you were a practicing private policeman!" Malcolm sighed.

Miss Ryder, very cross at all this, turned abruptly to the guess of honor: "Where did your sun god come from, Mrs. Malcolm?"

"You'd never, never guess! Would she, Johnny?"

"Never, never. Tell her."

"It came off a bandwagon!"

"A bandwagon?"

"A circus wagon."

"Well, I'll be hanged." Gamadge was amused. "That ought to take the blight off for you, Abby."

"It partly does," admitted Miss Ryder. "But where on earth did you find the circus wagon?"

"Well, as a matter of fact I only found that relic of it," said Redfield. "Many years ago, in a farmer's barn. I was looking for some seasoned pine I heard he had there, and in a corner, propped up among wagon wheels and old metal, was the god. It seems that a little traveling circus came to grief in that vicinity, in the Eighties, and disintegrated where it stood. The Apollo had been gilt and painted, and the farmer's father rescued it. Well he rather fascinated me; I saw him with his lyre in his hands, you know, tottering along in all his splendor, drawn by six white, caparisoned horses, to the strains of the calliope. In fact he may have been *on* the calliope. Well: he was now battered, in eclipse; but I couldn't resist him. I brought him home and stored him in the lumber room off the garage. I had had some vague idea of putting him up in the kitchen garden, among the sunflowers; but when my aunt here caught sight of him—she was on a tour of inspection, viewing the old domain and all its improvements—nothing would satisfy her but to establish him among the roses."

"I still think that was a mistake," said Miss Ryder "but I'm glad to find that it was only a mistake, and that you haven't gone crazy."

Cora Malcolm remarked that such a figure was a period piece, and that she'd rather like to see it.

"Has a little effect of something dug up, I must admit," confessed Redfield, "and I haven't promised my

dear Aunt Josephine—Vega—to keep it where it is forever. I'll store it after she goes, and trot it out again
when she comes back."

"You prefer a few field mice," said David Malcolm,
and his eyes, as they left Redfield's face, rested for a
moment, and for the first time, on Blanche Drummond's. Then they moved away.

She had been looking at the fire. Now she said, as
if with an effort, "You'd all love the Apollo if he
were an archaic ruin from Crete. Just because he's
representational—" Her voice died.

"Archaic!" said Vega. "That reminds me. Where
did you put that little antique thing I have for Cora,
Johnny?" And as Redfield got up and went over to a
Chinese cabinet, she continued, smiling at Cora Malcolm: "Just a souvenir, dear child. Something that
was your great-grandmother's."

The twins, polite and attentive, sat looking at her
inquiringly. Redfield, frowning a little, poked about
in a drawer of the cabinet and returned with a small
package done up in tissue paper. Vega took it from
him, unwrapped it, and held up a big, heart-shaped
gold brooch. Its surface, heavily embossed, was con-
vex; and on the raised center of the heart five little
stones were arranged like the petals of a flower. An
almost microscopic diamond sent forth a tiny ray
where the petals met.

"Did you ever see it, Cora?" Vega was looking at it
fondly.

"No, I can't say that I ever did."

"I thought you probably hadn't. It was with the
rest of the family jewelry, and when your mother
took you abroad to live she didn't of course take the
old things; and at that time you were so very young.

Your father"—she glanced down at the old-fashioned diamond ornament on her breast—"gave me the boxful when we were married. Of course you'll have everything when I'm gone, but I thought it would be nice for you to have this now. A token, you know." She smiled at Cora. "It was your great-grand-mother's—the Highlander. Her first husband was English, and he got this for her in London when they were engaged. There's a little secret to it. Your father showed it to me—see if *you* can find it."

Cora accepted the brooch, said that Mrs. Malcolm was very kind, and with her brother's assistance examined it. The secret was easily found; a little door, neatly contrived on the back of the ornament, disclosed when opened a fragment of something brown and faded under glass.

"Your great-grandfather's hair, of course," said Vega, "and that makes it a locket. Such exquisite workmanship! Do you see the little diamond in the center of the flower?"

Cora said she saw the little diamond. "And all the petals a different color. But why have three red ones?"

"One's dark red," said her brother, "and one's light red, and one's pink. Or pinkish. A tourmaline?"

"A tourmaline," repeated Cora. "And a ruby, I suppose, and an emerald and a garnet, and an amethyst. It's lovely. Thank you so much, Mrs. Malcolm," said Cora, glancing at the big cluster on Vega's breast.

The brooch was passed from hand to hand, and at last Cora took it from Gamadge's fingers and pinned it on the left-hand lapel of her coat.

"It's not the value," said Vega, looking incredibly smug, "it's the sentiment."

"A token," agreed Cora, in her low and expressionless voice.

Gamadge, looking at the pin, opened his mouth, closed it, and then sat with the slightly vacant air of one who has swallowed a remark.

Johnny got up. "It's just a trifle warm," he said. "I'll open the terrace doors." He went out into the hall, and presently a cool breeze brought with it into the living room a cawing of crows. "Confound those wretched birds," he said, coming back. "They've moved in on me this fall. George kept them down."

"I must confess," said Gamadge, "that there's nothing I like better than the cawing of crows on an autumn day; except the conversation of katydids. Both are pests; make something of that, if you like, somebody."

"What I make of it," said David Malcolm, "is that a perfect world would be lacking in delight."

A crow answered another from the depths of the garden. "Hang it, they're in the orchard," said Johnny.

David Malcolm murmured: "Oh for a rook rifle."

Johnny looked at him hopefully. "My boy, *would* you? There's an excellent substitute for a rook rifle in the cupboard under the stairs, a Winchester twenty-two. It was father's—you remember it, Vega? Always hanging ready in the hall in case someone sighted a chipmunk or a hawk, or heard a crow?"

"I remember," said Vega.

"And the ammunition's in the drawer of the hall table. But it's only a one-shot, David. Take several."

Malcolm went into the hall. A fine figure of a young man, after whom Vega gazed fondly. "He doesn't look as if he'd ever been wounded!" she declared.

"It was principally a head wound," said Cora. "His leg's all right now."

Malcolm returned, a shining brown rifle in his hands. "They don't make them any better," he said. "Anybody want to come down with me and try a shot at a crow?"

Blanche Drummond rose. She said: "I'll come," and walked across the room to him.

After a moment's pause Malcolm said: "All right. Anybody else?"

Nobody stirred. They went out into the hall together; and Walter Drummond was the only person in the room who did not watch them go.

"Your wife is really the most beautiful creature, Mr. Drummond," said Vega, "Quite dazzling. What did they call them in the old days in England? Professional beauties. I'm sure that they would have stood on chairs to see her. And the photographs in the shopwindows! Once I *saw* Mrs. Langtry. Lady Something then, and rather a stately ruin; but still going strong."

Her high laugh came on a perfect crescendo of cawing from the orchard, and in the ensuing silence the little clock on the mantel chimed musically and struck five.

3

Afternoon Stroll

Redfield was not one to sit helpless while an awkward pause prolonged itself. He said briskly: "Why don't we all stretch our legs? Stroll around the place? There's nothing to see in the gardens, of course, but there are a few things to pick, and Alice wants flowers for the house. I ought to collect some marigolds. How about it, Abby? Will you keep me company in the cutting garden?"

"I'll walk down with you, Johnny," said Abigail, getting up, "but I won't watch you cut marigolds. I hate the things. I hate the way they smell, and I hate that particular yellow."

"But they're such a sacred flower," protested Vega sentimentally.

"Let the Hindus hang them on the cows," said Abigail. "I'll take a walk around the Loop."

"Splendid. Just let me get my basket and the shears." Redfield and Abigail went out into the hall.

The others had risen. They stood irresolute for a few moments, until Walter Drummond said in his hesitating way: "We might help Redfield out, Miss Malcolm. I've got my pocketknife; what about going down and trying to find something? Zinnias? Cosmos?"

Cora Malcolm rose; a slim, strong figure, with dark hair cut short and thickly waved on her small head. "I'd like some exercise," she said. "I was thinking of croquet."

Johnny put his head in at the doorway. "By all means, Cora, if you can find partners. But the light will be fading. Don't forget the floodlamps in that tree in the orchard." He laughed. "I don't suppose anybody wants a swim!"

A chorus of protest answered him. He went off to join Abigail; Cora Malcolm and Drummond followed.

Vega glanced at Gamadge with amusement. "Well!" she said. "The Drummonds seem to have preëmpted my stepchildren."

"All very friendly," replied Gamadge, also smiling.

"And you've been left to take care of me. Shall we take a stroll too, Mr. Gamadge?"

"By all means. You must take me down to the shrine."

"The shrine? Oh, of course." She got up, shook out the flaring skirts of her robe, adjusted the yellow wreath, and walked beside him out to the terrace. Here she paused. "What a day! And to think that on such a day David is going to try to kill a living creature! I don't approve of any living creature being killed."

"Except by sunstroke?" asked Gamadge, and instantly regretted the question. He had no wish to make fun of anybody's religion, and it was just possible that the being at his side might actually entertain feelings of personal veneration for the sun. But she corrected him with such tolerance as she might have learned from her divinity, who shines impartially on the enthusiast and the skeptic:

"I meant killed by human beings, Mr. Gamadge. That interferes with the System. But natural deaths—they're part of the System; sunstroke, cyclones, earthquakes—if you understand?"

Gamadge said that he thought he did.

"And all this"—Vega threw back her head and lifted her arms to the sky with an air of proprietorship—"and all this"—she lowered the embrace to include her surroundings—"it's part of the System too."

"With a little landscaping superimposed," said Gamadge.

But from the terrace little of the landscaped grounds could be seen; they were hidden by the great wall of evergreens and birches that rose twenty feet away to conceal the rockery. To the left of the terrace, shrubbery masked the boundary fence and hedge that cut the property off from the lane which Gamadge and Miss Ryder had climbed that afternoon; to the right, shrubbery and trees—among them several enormous oaks—hid the parallel hedge and fence that divided the grounds of Idlers from the woods. Near the hedge on that side, not far from the southwest corner of the rockery, there was a little pavilion; and a gate in the hedge behind it led to a narrow path or trail which ran between woods and fence parallel to the lawn. The pavilion had once been a summerhouse, and was nicely ceiled and walled; now it was called the tool house; but it contained, besides garden implements, garden games—an archery set and a croquet set, and markers for clock-golf.

The lower slopes beyond the rockery were a succession of rectangles, running all the way from hedge to hedge, and themselves divided by six-foot hedges; they were connected by arches and wicket gates. First came a wide lawn, on the south side of which a rose garden, shut off by rustic posts and rose-vines, backed against the woods. Just below the rose garden on that side a wicket gate led from the lawn to outer precincts, a clearing in the woods where the trail from the tool house ended. This whole outer property, which included the greenhouse and the kitchen gardens, was encircled by the woods and by a well-kept road called the Loop; which provided the inmates of Idlers with an easy half-hour walk when they didn't care for rough hiking.

Below the lawn came the flower garden, which had a gate leading to the Loop; and below the flower garden was the orchard. Farthest down of all, in a wilder region, a swimming pool had been constructed from the old duck pond, and had a dam and a waterfall.

The rose garden could be approached through the rockery or around it on the south; but Vega preferred the rockery. Her sandals clip-clopped down the terrace steps, and when she and Gamadge had crossed the turf to the rockery path they clip-clopped again on the flags.

The rockery smelled damply sweet; it was deeply in shadow from the towering evergreens, and it had a stream and two cascades and pools. The second and larger of these, called the rock pool, was surrounded by a low wall. The path circled it.

As the two arrived at the rock pool, a crow cawed. Presently there was the crack of the rifle.

"Wonder if he got it," said Gamadge, stopping beside a big birch.

"I hope not," simpered Vega. "But don't tell Johnny I said so!"

They went on down stone steps, through a kind of tunnel formed by the trees and the shrubbery, and out on the lower lawn. Nobody was in sight. The rose garden, diagonally to their right, was now no more than a green square against the darker green of the woods behind it, but the vines, though blossomless, were still thick enough to form a screen impenetrable to sight. Even the wide, arched entrance was encroached upon by the hanging shoots, and by the branches that had grown out, unpruned, on both sides.

"Such a mass of color it was," said Vega, "not long ago."

A crow cawed, and the rifle cracked. Vega looked toward the arch that led into the flower garden below.

"I wonder if Cora and Mr. Drummond will find something down there," she said, "to reward them for their trouble."

Gamadge did not reply. There was complete silence now, except for the little sawing sound of the crickets. The breeze had fallen, shadows were lengthening, but the sun was still bright above the trees behind Idlers.

They entered the rose garden. All its paths were turfed, and a turf border ran between the outer beds and the trellis. There was a rustic bench in each corner; under the one to the left of the wooden statue lay a gardener's flat basket. It contained a pair of garden gloves and a weeding spud.

"That Wilson boy," complained Vega, "is always leaving his things about." They had arrived at the end of the middle path, and she stood in front of the image and smiled at Gamadge. "Well, here he is, Mr. Gamadge. Isn't he lovely?"

Gamadge looked at the god. The rounded base of the statue was broken, and the thing was supported— a little askew—by means of two pea sticks that ran from the middle of its back through the hedge and fence, down into the undergrowth beyond. Its outstretched hands were fingerless, half its raised left foot was gone, and except for the suggestion of a rudimentary nose and half a lip, it was faceless. Blackened where it had been gilded, worm-eaten and rain-sodden, its short tunic falling back from a knee that had weathered to a leprous gray, it did indeed look like something that had once been alive, and was now dead and exhumed.

"Lovely," said Gamadge.

"And isn't that a ray on his head?"

"Perhaps. At any rate, god or no god, he has his grove."

"His grove?"

Gamadge nodded towards the dark woods beyond the hedge. "They always had groves. The gods, you know."

"Did they? Then I must tell Johnny how right I was to insist on putting my Apollo here. And I shall certainly offer him some marigolds. Why should the Hindus have all the marigolds?"

David Malcolm's cool voice spoke from the archway: "I can offer him something he'll like better than marigolds, Mrs. Malcolm."

He stood there with Blanche Drummond, his rifle under his arm and two dead crows hanging from the fingers of his other hand; in that light, and against the green of the leaves, they looked like blocks of onyx.

"Good gracious, my dearest boy," cried Vega, "take those dreadful things away."

"But he'd like them. The Greeks were very tough very late, Mrs. Malcolm. Later than you think." He stood smiling, the crows swinging by their feet from his brown fingers. "And after all, if Apollo did destroy field mice—"

"Take them right away!"

Blanche said gaily: "We're going to hang them up beside the gate out there, so they won't dare to come in from the woods."

Malcolm was studying the wooden statue. Now he said: "I don't believe he's a god after all. He's probably Orpheus. Orpheus would be right for a bandwagon, and he had a cult, too—and what a cult! The Orphic mysteries—now they *were* something." He advanced, took the rifle from under his arm, and dropped it, butt down, within the outstretched arms. "Take care of it, old boy," he said, propping it against the broken foot, "it's loaded."

Gamadge said: "He may be Apollo; if so he oughtn't to have anything dangerous to play with. Surely you remember Hyacinthus?"

"And what happened to *him?*" asked Vega.

"Most unfortunate accident. He and Apollo were playing quoits—the discus, you know—and Apollo cast the discus in the wrong direction. It clove the young man's skull to the brain." Gamadge added firmly: "Interpreted by myth-breakers as sunstroke."

Vega looked pleased and scholarly.

"Well, the old boy doesn't know anything about guns," said Malcolm, "so I'll risk it."

He stepped across a rose-bed, pushed vines out of his way, and disappeared through the east wall of the trellis.

Blanche Drummond stood looking after him, and Gamadge wondered if it could really be Blanche who stood there so at a loss. He asked: "Did you account for one of those birds of prey, Blanche?"

"Oh—yes. I did." She looked at her gloves. "The rifle was oily. And dusty."

"Two shots, two crows. Bull's-eyes."

"Oh, they showed quite plainly up in the tree."

"Whereabouts?"

"In the orchard." But she was not diverted from her thoughts by Gamadge's attempt at small talk. She looked at the vines through which Malcolm had vanished. "I must go over to the greenhouse," she said, "and see whether there's anything there for Johnny." She followed in Malcolm's steps, parted the thorny creepers as he had done, and made an exit between the same two posts. The vines fell behind her like a curtain.

Vega stood looking after her for some moments. Then she remarked: "Well!"

"Just a short cut to the greenhouse," said Gamadge.

"I should like to drop a hint to that nice Mr. Drummond."

That nice Mr. Drummond, as she very well knew, was secluded with Cora Malcolm among the cosmos and the chrysanthemums; but no doubt Vega was one of those elderly ladies who judge the behavior of women more sternly than that of men.

She led the way out of the rose garden, across the lawn, and up to the rockery, chatting as they walked.

"It really isn't much more chilly for a swim today than it was at dawn this summer."

"At dawn?" Gamadge spoke with mild horror.

"There's nothing like a swim at dawn."

"Not for me. I never liked the dawn. To me it's eerie, very eerie indeed."

"Oh, but you miss so much in missing the dawn!"

"I'm too old now to learn anything new about the dawn," said Gamadge gloomily.

They climbed the rockery path to the pool. Vega walked halfway around it to stand against the big birch; with one hand she grasped a sapling, with the other she supported herself in an attitude of exalted abandonment by clutching the branch of a small, dying pine. Gamadge, on the other side of the pool, avoided contemplation of her by a study of frogs.

"I never know," he said, sitting on the low wall and bending to the water, "whether these are real frogs or some of Johnny's garden jokes. Not until they—"

The one he was looking at solved the problem by leaping from his ledge and entering the water with a plop. Gamadge took out his handkerchief and wiped his face.

"Wood life is full of hazards at all times," he observed, "but at dawn—who knows what goes on at dawn? Transformations. The things that were sitting on the toadstools jump away, and objects that had come to life become inanimate again. Your idol, for instance. I hope—"

"You are absurd, Mr. Gamadge," said Vega, her face raised to the sunlight that filtered down from an opening in the treetops. "Fear is not in the System."

"It's crept in somehow. That frog didn't jump off

his perch when my shadow touched him because he loved me."

"All that is a mistake; just a mistake. My stepchildren, now: they don't like me."

"Young people are often brusque nowadays."

"At least they'll take my money now."

Gamadge looked up at her, but her face was inscrutable.

"And they'll have it all," she went on, "when I've been absorbed into the System."

Gamadge, who felt rather like a kobold disputing with an eccentric fairy, so deeply was he in shadow, so brightly did the sun touch her beaky face and her yellow dress, shook his head. "Absorption? That sounds very easy and peaceful. Have you definite information about the process in your own case?"

"I have information."

"You wouldn't care to pass the information along to me?"

"You wouldn't understand. It takes years of study."

"That's where you metaphysicians have it all over the rest of us," began Gamadge, and then the rifle cracked.

"I didn't hear a crow, did you?" he asked, still bending over another frog that he thought must certainly be an iron one. Then, getting no reply, he looked up. Vega stood against the big birch, supported by her grasp of the sapling and the little pine; there seemed to be a fly on her forehead, and as Gamadge looked, it seemed to begin to crawl downwards. He leapt up at the moment the body plunged, but before he reached it it lay across the ledge of the pool. The yellow wreath had fallen off, and floated on the dark water.

4

Autumn Flowers

The dead woman was big-boned and heavy; it took
Gamadge a minute or two to get her off the wall, and
to lay her down on the mossy earth of the rockery.
She had been shot squarely between the eyes, and the
bullet had not emerged.

He stood up, turned, and backed against the trunk
of the big birch. He was facing as Vega had done,
along the rockery path and out upon the lawn, and
he knew at once that pursuit of the murderer would
be useless. Forty yards down and diagonally to the
right, the lower angle of the rose garden, like a section of green wall, cut into his line of vision. Within
that section the rifle must have been fired. Even if the
murderer had not known that Gamadge was in the off-
ing, concealed for the moment behind shrubs, to stand
and fire outside the rose garden in the open would
have meant a lunatic risk of being seen.

The rifle had been fired from within the angle of
the enclosure; and before Gamadge had raised the
body the murderer had escaped from the upper or
the lower side of the place. In whichever direction
Gamadge ran he might find someone; he was pretty
sure that the party was scattered, otherwise the murderer would not have risked the crime at all, and the

chance of mutual alibis; but where was Gamadge to look for a killer?

Escape had been made to the upper grounds, through the gate behind the tool house; or it had been made by way of the gate in the south hedge, now concealed by the angle of the rose garden, and up through the woods or down the Loop. From the Loop it was only a few yards to the greenhouse or the vegetable gardens, only a few yards into the flower garden, and thence to the orchard and the swimming pool below.

Gamadge looked at his watch—twenty-eight minutes past five. The shot had been fired at least two minutes earlier. He got out his handkerchief and covered the dead woman's face; then he walked down the flagged steps and out on the lawn.

There was not a soul in sight, and hardly a sound except the sawing of the crickets. The greens were vivid in this waning light, and every leaf and twig of the hedges picked out as if by an old-fashioned artist with an eye for detail. He went into the rose garden. Yes: there, in the left-hand corner, lay the rifle; and beside it the garden gloves that he had seen in the basket a few minutes before. There also was the weeding spud; it lay near a heap of piled turf—small, neat squares that had very recently been removed from their bed.

They were lying at different levels, and when he stepped carefully around them, bent sideways, and peered through the vines, he saw that they were exactly beneath the area through which the muzzle of the rifle must have been pushed and aimed. He could see the big birch.

But he couldn't swear to Vega's exact position

against it, and the bullet hadn't come out through the back of her head and marked the spot where she had stood. An inch to right or left—that would make a difference here. The murderer's mind had worked furiously, but it had worked accurately. Time had been taken before the murder to pile these squares of sod so that no expert would be able to determine the exact line of fire, and from it the height of the marksman.

The killer had known that a bullet from a .22 probably wouldn't emerge from the back of a human skull.

Gamadge bent over the heaps of sod; Drummond, Malcolm or himself might have fired from ground level, to the right or left. Blanche might have fired from one level, Redfield or Cora Malcolm from two, Abigail from the third. If they were all tested, any fractional discrepancy would be accounted for by the personal idiosyncrasy of each—under strain—in holding the gun.

And unless the garden gloves had been available the murder probably wouldn't have been committed. There would not only be lack of time after the murder to rub off fingerprints, but all these people knew that the hand that fires a rifle may show evidence of having done so. Blanche Drummond already wore gloves, and had fired the rifle while wearing them; she would use these large cotton things over her own to widen the field of suspicion. Malcolm's hands might be stained; but he would certainly have used the gloves, for the same reason.

Gamadge went out of the enclosure, to see Walter Drummond coming through the gate in the tall hedge that cut off the flower garden from the lawn.

"Hello," called Drummond. "Johnny's dahlias are dead." He carried a great bunch of russet-brown button chrysanthemums.

Gamadge asked: "Where's Miss Malcolm? Not with you?"

"She only stayed with me a few minutes. She was saying something about croquet."

"I remember."

"There's a sporting layout down in the orchard." He jerked his head backwards.

"Is she in the orchard?" asked Gamadge.

"No, she went up to the tool house where the set is. She didn't come through again." He added: "What have you done with the old lady?"

"Abigail?"

Drummond, looking shocked, said of course not. Mrs. Malcolm. He added with a laugh: "If that was a reconciliation party this afternoon, give me w-war to the knife." He stammered a little when he was nervous. "Kids won't get their money," he said, "if they go on like that."

"Anybody pass through the flower garden while you were there? After your wife and Malcolm came up with the crows?"

"I didn't even see them. I was behind that bank of cosmos at the other end."

"Behind the cosmos for half an hour?" Gamadge looked at his watch. "You left the house before five. It's five thirty-five now."

"What of it?" Drummond's sunburned face was frowning. "What is it to you how long I've been there?" He added: "Plenty to see in a garden, even at this time of the year."

Mrs. Drummond came through the gate from the

Loop. She had a few red and white carnations in her hand. "Nothing but these in the place," she said, "nothing at all. Oh—you found something, Walter. Good. We might ask Johnny for a few. Ours are so poor."

Drummond replied: "Johnny hasn't more than enough for himself."

"Have you been picking pinks all this long time, Blanche?" asked Gamadge.

"Long time? What do you mean? It wasn't long, was it?"

"He's got some game," said Drummond, "timing us all."

Cora Malcolm came slowly down from the upper grounds, past the end of the rockery. There was a croquet mallet in her hand; she was swinging it. When she was abreast of the entrance to the rose garden she paused. "Anybody want a game?" she asked.

"Have you been up in the tool house all this time, Miss Malcolm?" asked Gamadge, turning to look at her.

"I sat on the steps after I got out my lucky mallet, and had a cigarette."

Blanche cried: "You've lost your gold pin, Cora!"

Cora glanced down at her left lapel. "It does seem to have fallen off," she said. "The catch was old and loose."

"No wonder you look terrified! Your stepmother will have a fit," remarked Blanche, arranging her carnations.

"I can find it. I know where I've been." Cora did not look terrified, but neither did she look happy. All her ironical gaiety was gone. She faced the entrance to the rose garden. "I really must," she said, "see that Apollo thing."

Gamadge said: "You see it now, Miss Malcolm."

"What a horror. I must see it close."

"Don't think of going into the place."

She glanced over her shoulder at him. "Verboten?"

"I might almost say polizeilich verboten."

"Man's crazy," said Drummond. "He has some game on."

"Perhaps he thinks the place is uncanny," said Cora, gazing in at the statue. "It ought to be."

Redfield came through the gate from the Loop, his basket overflowing with marigolds. He shut the gate behind him and latched it. "I don't know," he said, "why none of you can close a gate. A gate is supposed to be meant to keep things out, you know; and this one actually does do something about the rabbits."

"I won't shoot rabbits for you, Mr. Redfield," said David Malcolm, who now sauntered through the gate from the flower garden. "I love the bunnies." He was carrying a bunch of wild asters.

Gamadge was looking at Redfield. He asked: "Where's Abigail?"

"Went around the Loop. Wanted a stroll."

"How long ago?"

"My God," said Drummond, "he's at it again."

Redfield said that Abby had only been with him a minute or so. "She ought to be back any time now." He looked from Drummond to Malcolm. "Well!" he exclaimed. "I must say I'm obliged to you for those flowers. And so will Alice be. But I'm under a double obligation to you, David, because you shot me a couple of crows. I saw them hanging up."

Blanche Drummond said: "I shot one of them, Johnny."

"Good! All that target practice wasn't for nothing, then. I'm glad to know it. One's peace was shattered all summer, but not in vain. Where did you get those asters, David? They're a lovely blue."

"I got them down by the swimming pool."

"Mighty thoughtful of you. Where's your stepmother?" He swung about to take in the emptiness of the farther landscape. "Did she go back to the house, Gamadge?"

Miss Ryder came through the wicket gate, and closed it carefully behind her.

"That's right, Abby!" Redfield smiled at her. "*You* wouldn't leave a gate open."

"Why should I?" She advanced, and Gamadge realized, seeing the red spray of false Solomon's-seal in her hand, that she at least required no alibi. She would never have required one from him, now she was clear in the eyes of the law.

Johnny at least could verify this. "We know where *you've* been," he went on. "There's only one place where those grow in my woods."

Gamadge knew the place; a shadowed spot, on the far side of the Loop and some distance off the road. He said: "You couldn't have been with Johnny long; that's a fact."

"I'm sorry to tell you, Abigail," said Blanche Drummond in a tone of regret, "that while you've been away your cousin Henry has quietly gone mad. He wants to know where we've all been, and how long we were there, and why."

Miss Ryder, acquainted with Gamadge's "plodding" ways, was a little taken aback. She gave him a sharp glance. What she saw in his face did not reassure her; she asked quickly: "What is it?"

He had stepped back; the others were now in front of him, and formed a ragged semicircle; with David Malcolm at the left end of it and his sister near the entrance to the rose garden on the right. Gamadge said: "I've been waiting until you were all here. Hang on to yourself, Abby; bad news. Mrs. Malcolm is dead."

Cora Malcolm broke the ensuing blank silence. She swung to face him, and with a gesture toward the rose garden, asked: "In *there?*"

"No. Up beyond the rock pool."

The Malcolms looked across the arc of the semicircle at each other; their features were rigid. Johnny Redfield came to life:

"You mean—Gamadge! What . . . ? Heart failure? A stroke?" He dropped the basket of marigolds and began to run up the lawn.

Gamadge called after him: "Redfield—don't go."

"Not go? What do you—"

"She was killed. Somebody shot her with the rifle." He nodded towards the rose garden. "In there; somebody shot her from in there."

Johnny stood with his arms hanging; he looked dazed and incredulous. Drummond said: "Good Lord; I heard it—a third shot. I thought . . ." He turned his head to stare at David Malcolm.

Malcolm's lips curved into a faint smile. He said: "Not me."

Johnny gasped: "Some fool picked up the gun and shot at a crow or something. Accident. David—you left the rifle somewhere?"

"Yes," said Malcolm. "I did."

"My God. We're in for—" He started up the slope again.

Gamadge said: "Johnny, wait a minute. Don't you understand? Nobody's owned up."

Redfield halted again. He looked over his shoulder. "Owned up?"

"Nobody's going to take the blame."

Redfield slowly turned and came back. "I don't—oh. Yes. I see. But nobody *knew*—until this minute." He looked from face to face. "I can hardly take it in myself. Where was she? Did you see it happen, Gamadge?"

"Not quite. I looked up a few seconds later, and saw her fall. She had been standing in front of the big birch. She was in plain sight from that corner of the place in there. Johnny, it wasn't an accident."

Blanche Drummond cried out: "Of course it was! It must have been. What else could it be? I know what happened, Johnny; the Wilson boy came back for something. He's only fifteen; it's just what a boy would do—see a rifle and snatch it up, and never wait to find out if it was loaded. And point it at the first thing, and pull the trigger."

Gamadge said: "Then the Wilson boy waited to put gloves on, Blanche, and piled up sods of turf to stand on."

Johnny faltered: "Piled up sods?"

"Were sods piled up before?"

"I can't imagine what you mean. No sods are piled anywhere now. We started cutting in this nearest corner, but my old occasional man couldn't manage it after all." He turned to Blanche. "For heaven's sake don't spread such stuff about the Wilson boy, Blanche. He isn't here on Sundays."

"We can soon settle the whereabouts of the Wilson boy, I hope," said Gamadge.

"Yes. But the thing is now"—again Redfield started for the rockery—"I can't let her lie there, Gamadge. Not another moment."

"Johnny"—Gamadge's tone halted him again—"you know you can't touch her until the police come. In a few minutes you can get something and cover her; but now—don't you see? It's our one chance."

"To do what?" shouted Redfield.

"To try to eliminate some of the crowd before the police do come. To keep what names we can off the record. Once they're on it, and the papers get them—nobody ever forgets. But if we can find out where everybody was, and what they were doing, and whom they saw . . ."

Redfield took out his handkerchief and wiped his face. "This is ghastly." He looked at his guests, a pleading look. "Of course it was an accident. I understand—the unfortunate party is flabbergasted for the moment. But now—we're civilized people. We can't let anybody else take the blame. I mean the unfortunate party can't. Nobody'll think the worse of anybody—hunting and shooting accidents happen all the time. We'll all stand by."

Silence answered him.

Gamadge said: "You see how it is, Johnny. I'll take the responsibility for the delay—just a few minutes."

Drummond turned again to Malcolm, whose dark face was inscrutable. Drummond himself, big and bony, redheaded and red-faced, stolid and taciturn, was far the more typical Scot of the two. He asked: "Where did you leave the damned thing?"

Blanche Drummond broke in shrilly: "In the rose

garden. We came up here and heard voices and went in to show the dead crows. Mrs. Malcolm was there with Henry; Henry saw us—saw David give the rifle to the statue."

"Saw him do what?" Redfield gaped at her.

"Give the rifle to that wooden statue. Henry saw him."

"Yes," said Malcolm, in his low, pleasant, uninflected voice, "and warned me, too."

5

Joking Aside

"We could joke about the rifle half an hour ago," said Gamadge. "Now we must—"

"Just one moment." David Malcolm stood in an easy posture, one hand in a pocket, the other gently swishing the long sheaf of wild asters against his leg. There was a half-smile on his lips, but under this appearance of cool assurance a close observer would have seen tautness and control.

"Yes, Mr. Malcolm?"

"Do I understand that you were *with* Mrs. Malcolm?"

"Every moment, although I didn't happen to have my eyes on her at the moment she died."

"Then excuse me for asking: why exactly do you feel yourself in a position to conduct an inquiry? I mean—even assuming that you had no motive for killing my stepmother, and no animus against her, you did, so far as the rest of us know, have time to do pretty much as you liked afterwards in the rose garden. Not that I suppose you would manipulate evidence in favor of—say—any old friend; at the expense—say—of newer acquaintances. But the fact that you had opportunity does rather remove you from the rôle of purely disinterested observer, doesn't it?

Taken in connection with your entirely natural bias, you know."

Redfield, his face screwed into an expression of vexed impatience, spluttered: "My dear boy, I beg of you, don't make an ass of yourself! Motive? Animus? It's only by the merest chance that Gamadge ever came up this afternoon, or ever met my poor aunt at all. As for bias—tampering with evidence—shocking nonsense! He wants to find out who's responsible for this tragedy, since nobody *takes* the responsibility! We couldn't get a better man to do it. For God's sake, David, don't obstruct! It—it doesn't *look* well."

Malcolm, still smiling, said: "I note the cautionary implication of what you say. Let the expert in murder proceed."

Gamadge, who had seemed to ignore this passage, went on equably:

"Check me at any point. What I am about to say may elicit protest from Mr. Malcolm, but Redfield will probably back me. My cousin Abigail is accounted for and eliminated." He nodded towards Abby, who stood square and firmly planted, distress on her face and the spray of false Solomon's-seal in her hand. "Redfield will say whether he has ever seen false Solomon's-seal at any point in these woods nearer than the far side of the Loop."

"No, I haven't," said Redfield. "There isn't any, except in that clearing off the road, beside the stream."

"If my cousin picked the spray there," continued Gamadge, "she couldn't have been in the rose garden at five twenty-six, which I will call the time when the tragedy occurred. I certainly wasn't more than two minutes in getting Mrs. Malcolm off the edge of the pool, and laying her down in front of the big birch up there; than I looked at my watch, and it was five twenty-eight. Give Abby five minutes—a short estimate—to get down to the vegetable gardens and get off on her walk. Call it then seven minutes past five. Assume that the person who fired the rifle spent five minutes in the rose garden before the rifle was fired; I think that's fair—those turfs had to be dug up and arranged. That gives my cousin fourteen minutes to get to the clearing beside the stream and back again. She couldn't do it. I couldn't do it in fourteen, whichever way I went. She was back here at about five-forty, and that's when she would normally be back after a walk around the Loop—a good half-hour."

Drummond said angrily: "You don't have to go through all that. Of course Miss Ryder's out of it."

"Of course," said Blanche. "Ridiculous."

"I don't want any favors," said Abigail.

"You don't need any, Miss Ryder," said Malcolm, smiling, "so far as I'm concerned."

"My cousin is of no use to us as a witness, either," continued Gamadge, "because she wasn't here. She couldn't have seen who went or came at twenty minutes past five, Miss Malcolm."

As he swung to her she started violently. She had not moved away from her position in front of the rose garden; she had been standing motionless, the croquet mallet held loosely in her hand. Now, lifting her head to face him, she paused a moment; then she said: "Yes?"

"You and Walter Drummond left the house shortly before five o'clock. You came down to the flower garden this way?" He gestured towards the gate below him and on his left.

"Yes."

"You were with him there only a few minutes. You then left by the gate that opens on the Loop? I assume so, since Mrs. Malcolm and I didn't see you as we came down."

"Yes; I went out that way." She looked at Abigail. "Miss Ryder was just disappearing around the bend, where the road goes under the trees."

"You came up past the rose garden, through the woods."

"Yes. I heard Mrs. Malcolm's voice there."

"But not your brother's; he hadn't arrived yet. You must have gone up to the tool house, then, by way of that upper gate."

"I did."

"It didn't occur to you to stop by and see the Apollo *then?*"

"No. Mrs. Malcolm was there, as I said."

"Shoals, 'ware shoals, Cora," said her brother, smiling at her.

"That's very silly, David." She returned his look gravely. "Nobody here imagines that we liked her."

"Sensible of you, Miss Malcolm," said Gamadge, "to admit the obvious."

"I'm not at all sure," said Malcolm, "that either of us ought to admit anything."

"David, my boy," said Redfield imploringly, "how often must I tell you—"

"You needn't tell me again, Mr. Redfield."

Gamadge turned again to Cora Malcolm. "So, not caring to have to converse with the deceased, you passed us by. And then you settled down in the tool house for the next twenty-five minutes or so?"

"It didn't seem a long time to me. I got out a croquet mallet, and looked around at things, and then I sat on the steps smoking."

"That third shot must have sounded pretty close?"

"I didn't pay much attention to it. I knew David and Mrs. Drummond would get all the crows they had light to see."

"But in fact they gave up the chase when they had shot two. Walter: you say you didn't leave the flower garden after Miss Malcolm left you, until I met you coming out of it at five thirty-five."

"No; I didn't."

"And you didn't see anybody come through—or go through—because you were behind the dahlias and the cosmos. You didn't see your wife and Malcolm come up from the orchard, and you didn't see Malcolm return for his trip down to the swimming pool."

"No, I didn't."

"Johnny. You were picking marigolds; I suppose you saw nobody? Not Miss Malcolm walking up the Loop, not Blanche Drummond crossing to the greenhouse? Not Mr. Malcolm hanging up crows?"

Redfield had shaken his head after each suggestion. He now spoke with a kind of irritated apology: "No, and I can't help it if I didn't. I was grubbing at big weeds. I was back there behind the sunflowers. I was at the far end of the place, and it's big."

"It's big. Blanche—"

She cried almost angrily: "Henry, I went straight to the greenhouse, and I stayed there. I was looking at Johnny's plants and wondering what he'd have next spring. It wasn't long. It couldn't have been long. I hardly heard that third shot at all. The rifle was right there, and I thought somebody had picked it up and just fired at something. There might have been a crow right on the top of one of those posts. The time *goes* when you're looking at things in a greenhouse."

"Twenty minutes went, at least. Mr. Malcolm."

Malcolm, again gently swishing the sheaf of asters against his leg, replied: "Mr. Gamadge."

"We talked to you in the rose garden. You went out of it to hang up crows, I presume that you saw Mrs. Drummond afterwards, since she followed you almost immediately."

"I saw her to speak to."

"Of course he saw me," said Blanche. "On my way to the greenhouse. I didn't think you wanted me to mention that."

"You might mention now whether you saw him walk up or down the road afterwards."

"I never noticed."

"I walked down the road," said Malcolm, "past this gate and on down to the lower gate. I went through the flower garden to the archway that leads into the orchard, and I went through the orchard and down to the swimming pool. I didn't see Mr. Redfield in the vegetable garden as I went past; he was behind the sunflowers. I didn't see Mr. Drummond in the flower garden as I cut across to the orchard; he was behind the cosmos. I didn't see a soul. I cut these things"—he lifted the wild asters, looked at them, and dropped his arm—"and then I came back through the orchard and across the corner of the flower garden and along the turf path around to the gate that leads to this lawn. And I didn't see a soul that time, either."

"Drummond was already here by that time."

"So he was."

"Well then." Gamadge's eyes left him, to rest suc-

cessively on the other faces that were turned to his.
"The evidence is now at hand. . . . What must
we conclude from it? We must conclude—if the
witnesses are all to be believed—that somebody got
in."

The faces confronting him expressed an almost lu-
dicrous astonishment.

"It's not physically impossible, is it Johnny?" asked
Gamadge. "Some enemy of Mrs. Malcolm's *could*
have come into the grounds, overheard the talk about
the rifle in the rose garden, watched to see where
Mrs. Malcolm went, and seized the opportunity?"

Redfield, his face clearing a little, said after a pause
that it was certainly possible. "Of course the only way
to get in is by the front," he explained slowly.
"There's no back way except the gate from our lane
down there to the swimming pool; but that's pad-
locked, and I'm the only one that has a key. We're
completely wired until you come out on the drive.
But the servants were all busy in the house this afternoon, and there's nobody in the garage now." He
looked greatly puzzled. "Somebody could get by," he
admitted, his words dragging. "I hope to God they
did."

"It's the picture we're offering to the police," said
Gamadge. "Our private investigation has collapsed;
nobody saw anybody, nobody has an alibi, and so far
as we're concerned, Mrs. Malcolm wasn't killed at all.
We must suggest an outsider; in which case the inquiry will be based on motive—or mania.

"But can we suggest our outsider's method of escape? It was touch and go, you understand; I might
have run after the murderer without stopping to find
out whether Mrs. Malcolm was dead or not. I had

forty yards to run, but I can't see that the outsider would have had twenty. Up into the woods—a step. Down to the flower garden—a few yards. Across to the picking garden or the greenhouse—" He smiled. "Excuse me; I must include all possibilities, you know—twenty yards. Circuitous route through the lower and south woods, back to the front drive—easy.

"And of course it's for the police to resolve the difficulties: the coincidences, and the failure of our outsider to be seen by us.

"Johnny, whom do we call? The sheriff at Old Bridge?"

Johnny mumbled: "Old fellow. I don't think . . . Gamadge!"

"Johnny?"

"The police—they won't go after an outsider simply because we tell them to!"

"No, of course not. They have no tact; they can't afford tact. They won't respect our feelings—they're not allowed to, in a murder case. Here we are, six suspects, if my cousin Abigail is out of it. She won't be, until they've combed the woods for false Solomon's-seal. They'll fix on the rifle, you know. I mean they'll ask who knew it was in the rose garden.

"I knew it was there, Blanche Drummond and Mr. Malcolm knew it was there. Unless others hung about the place and heard us talking about it—rather cryptically, too—the others, Miss Malcolm and you and Drummond, didn't know where it was.

"Why should they have hung about the place? Well, Miss Malcolm had earlier expressed interest in the Apollo, and she herself tells us that she heard voices in the rose garden. Drummond might have finished cutting his flowers, wandered up to see what the rest of us were doing. You might have had some errand in the place.

"And to any of you retreat would, as I have said before, been safe, and safer because you all had flowers in your hands—except Miss Malcolm, who still carries her croquet mallet. Innocent occupations, and convincing enough to *us*. I rush down here and through the wicket gate; and I see somebody approaching with a bunch of flowers. I rush to the flower garden, and I see Walter and his chrysanthemums. I rush up the slope, and I meet Miss Malcolm, ready for her game.

"Now we must call the sheriff, Redfield."

Redfield said wearily: "The sheriff won't do. State police barracks outside of Rivertown. We'd better have them. Call Griggs, Gamadge; Griggs knows us. I'm going up to the rockery to stay with *her*. I shan't touch her, Gamadge, but I'm going to stay there till they come."

Abigail walked across to join them. "I'll go with you, Johnny."

"Thanks, Abby. You would."

As they went off Blanche Drummond asked: "Henry, can I go home?"

"Blanche, you must know you can't."

"Well, I suppose I can go up to the house."

"Certainly."

She went up the lawn, past the rose garden, past the thick shrubbery on her right that concealed the rockery, on to the house. Malcolm waited until she had gone, and then reached his sister in long strides. She looked as if she might sink to the grass, but he put an arm about her shoulders. They followed Blanche.

Gamadge said: "You'll have to telephone, Walter. I must stay down here."

Drummond had been looking after the Malcolms. He collected himself, and went up the lawn as far as the rose garden. But there he stopped and turned.

"Gamadge," he said explosively, "we're all more concerned in this than you are, and I'm a lawyer, and I'm familiar with sporting rifles. We had to take your word for it about conditions in there." He jerked his head. "The police will have to take your word for it. Ought to have another opinion."

"Well, Walter," said Gamadge cheerfully, "that can only mean that you think I may go in there again and alter something. I don't know why you should think that, but I agree with you that you may as well see the place as it is and check up on my description. I'll go in with you."

Drummond stood looking at him.

"You can't mean," said Gamadge, "that you want to go in alone? What would that do to the evidence? Do you want to tell the police, and state at the inquest, that you insisted on going in there alone?"

Drummond stood obstinately where he was, scowling.

"Well," said Gamadge, taking a cigarette, "I can't stop you. You'd make two of me in cross section. But I think we ought to keep the record clear as far as possible, and as it is I can swear that since I was there nothing has been tampered with, nothing planted, and nothing taken away. And I can also swear, and I don't think I'll be challenged on that point, that I haven't an earthly tie—except old acquaintance—with anybody in the case except Abby."

Drummond stood irresolute; the heads of the chrysanthemums that he still carried trailed on the grass.

"I'll tell you what," said Gamadge. "I'll call to Abby—she won't mind telephoning the state police. Then we can both stay here until they come."

Drummond opened and closed his free hand.

"And I may add," said Gamadge, "that I don't think they'll find I missed anything."

Drummond, without another word, turned and walked up the lawn. Gamadge watched him go; then he went and sat down against one of the entrance posts of the rose garden. He was far from comfortable; the sun-baked ground was hard, rose thorns made themselves felt through the back of his coat, and a chill breeze came up as the sun went down. But he stayed where he was until a young state policeman, gun in hand, came down the slope from the house.

"You Mr. Gamadge?"

"I am." Gamadge rose with alacrity.

"Lieutenant Griggs wants to see you up at the house. And county's here—Mr. Mosson." He came past Gamadge, and looked into the rose garden. "Jeeps!" he exclaimed. "What's that?"

"That is a garden decoration."

"Was that thing what was holding the rifle?"

"Yes."

"My oh my."

"Are you staying down here, Officer, until the experts come?"

"Right here. They'll be slow, it's Sunday."

"Everything happens on Sunday," said Gamadge, dusting off mown grass and twigs. "Have you noticed?

Toothaches; and refrigerators break down, and fuses blow."

"And there's murder on the routes, only it always comes out manslaughter or unavoidable accident."

"Might I ask if you're going in there, Officer?"

"I am if I want to disobey orders."

"Do you?"

"No."

"I won't presume to warn you that there just might be footprints somewhere."

"Lieutenant Griggs had the same idea."

Gamadge went off up the slope, but when he reached the upper corner of the rose garden he paused and looked over his shoulder. Seeing that the officer was staring fixedly into the enclosure, quite fascinated by Apollo, he turned left instead of going on to the house.

Halfway along the west side of the garden he swung right and went through shrubbery to the tool house. Hands in pockets, head a little down, he looked the very picture of an idler lost in meditation; but he was retracing the paths that might have been taken by a murderer.

He stopped at the tool house steps to look at Cora Malcolm's cigarette end and burnt match, which lay in the grass beside them; he went into the tool house, and wandered about there. He looked into the open box which contained the croquet set; the red mallet wasn't there, of course, but the red ball was. She hadn't taken that.

He came out again, passed behind the tool house and through the gate into the woods, and went down the trail that led to the Loop. He paused at a spot behind the rose garden where the hedge was thin, where he could see Apollo. The props supporting him came through the fence and disappeared in a wide strip of brushwood and dead leaves. Gamadge stood for a moment gazing at the averted figure of the sun god, at the fold of tunic where the green props fitted so securely. A bare shoulder emerged from the tunic; so pitted and scarred it was, such an ugly gray, that it was less like wood than like a fragment of abandoned wasp's nest. He turned away and went on down the trail to the Loop.

He followed it down to the lower gate that led into the flower garden, not turning aside to visit the greenhouse or the kitchen gardens; went through the gate, and along a path to the high wall of cosmos. He passed behind this, and returned to the gate by the path that skirted the orchard. He did not go into the orchard.

Retracing his way, he came out behind the tool house; cut from that point to the side lawn, and in the fading light reached the terrace steps.

6

Gouch

Lieutenant Griggs of the Rivertown state police had a short, square face which seldom showed other expression than a granite calm. But although the daylight lamp on Redfield's studio worktable did not light up his features, which were in shadow, the shadow was not deep enough to hide the fact that the lieutenant's brow was furrowed.

There were three comfortable couches in the studio, one flanking either end of the fireplace, in which a fire burned, and one beneath the east windows. Redfield lay on this last, his eyes closed and his pose one of exhaustion. Gamadge sat on the couch to the left of the hearth, and on the other, facing him, sat Mr. Ellsworth Mosson, State's Attorney of Rivertown.

The studio was a splendid room, with a big rounded window along its south wall, and casement windows to the east and west. Redfield said that it was the only studio on earth which had no north light, but then his work could be done in any light; he seldom used color. There was color, though, in a delightful flower piece, done in opaque tints on gray paper, that hung over the mantel. Bold and stylized without being too mannered, it was Redfield at his best.

He had at first intended the studio to be neutral in tone, and its decorative scheme was based on an arrangement of black, white, and silver; but when it came to furnishings his earlier taste for color had triumphed. The curtains and upholstery had somehow ended by blooming with big red roses, while one interesting note was struck by a large armchair in violent blue.

There were small tables in front of the fire, one holding a bottle of whisky, a siphon, and a bowl of ice, besides Mr. Mosson's highball. The other stood at Gamadge's elbow, and upon it stood *his* highball. Redfield's glass was in his hand. Lieutenant Griggs refused to drink while investigating a case on the premises.

He said, looking at his clasped hands, "It ought to be an accident. I wish it was an accident. But it wasn't, Mr. Redfield. That bullet came out of that twenty-two, and Mr. Gamadge was right about where it was fired from. He was right about those piled turfs, too; they were fresh out of the ground. Any of the people there could have fired that shot, but we can leave Miss Ryder out of it. Unless"—he smiled gloomily—"our men do find any of those red berries on the place nearer than where you all say she picked them."

"They don't grow on her little place down the hill," said Gamadge, also smiling a little. "And I don't in any case think she brought them along with her in her pocket."

"Thank goodness," said Mosson, who was a lank, tow-headed, normally cheerful man without illusions of any kind. "The thought of Abby Ryder as a murder suspect really is not bearable."

"She'd play up," said Gamadge. "And so will I, if you like."

"Oh, for mercy's sake stay out of it," said Mosson. "We have too many people in it now. Unless you're secretly developing homicidal mania? No? Then stay out of it. How about you, Redfield?" He cast a faintly incredulous look at the figure supine on the couch under the east windows. "Any chance of leaving you out?"

"No," said Redfield with his eyes shut. "There isn't. Even I could have shot my aunt Josephine with that Winchester—forty yards is practically point-blank range. I've shot crows. And I had a financial motive, too. I'm her residuary legatee, at least I was the last I heard of it. She's made a new will, lately, I understand, leaving some money to some astrological society or other—perhaps as a sop to their sensibilities; she was losing interest in them. But I don't think she'd leave them much. I don't get a cent of the Malcolm money, of course; but last spring she had about seven thousand in the bank, and since she's been here she's had two income installments—early in July and early in October. They amount to about twelve thousand apiece. So I may now come in for something like thirty thousand gross, say, and perhaps I needed it. You never can tell. I'm not conscious of needing it as badly as all that, but you can check up on me. I do most of my business with the old Chemists in New York, but I keep a pretty good balance at Old Bridge. You can check up on me for blackmail or the double life. And I paid out a mysterious little aggregate of

forty-seven dollars last spring; it went to my bookie, if
you must know."

Mosson said: "Thk thk."

"Griggs has her checkbooks," continued Redfield
wearily. "I'll give you the name of her bank in Los
Angeles. I haven't their number.

"But perhaps you ought to know that I preferred
her to live. I was fond of her—I had reason to be.
Apart from the fact that she was an inoffensive
woman and had always been most kind to me otherwise, she'd been giving me five thousand a year ever
since she got her income, after old Malcolm died. For
ten years she's been giving it to me yearly to keep the
old place up. Now—I don't know."

Griggs looked at him, rather awed: "Five thousand
a year!"

"It doesn't go so very far, Griggs, especially
nowadays." Redfield smiled at him. "But it made the
difference. Any man who says that five thousand a
year doesn't make a difference, that man's a liar. She
had a sentiment about the old place, though she
never came near it until this summer since before she
was married; and she had a sentiment for me." He
smiled again. "I'm the last of the Redfields."

"She had forty-eight thousand dollars' income?"
asked Mosson.

"Just about, after taxes were paid. You'll find it all
in her checkbook."

"But only for life."

"Only for life."

"But she had, say, thirty thousand in the bank,
which if she didn't leave it away from you in this last
will, comes to you."

"Yes. It ought to be nearly that. She didn't spend a

cent of those two installments here—had plenty of cash with her. Sent the checks right back to Los Angeles for deposit."

"Well," said Mosson, "all I can say is that if you killed her for thirty-odd thousand, you were a damned fool. The medical examiner seems to think she was a pretty good insurance risk. You might have got a hundred thousand from her before she died a natural death."

Griggs said: "There's a big difference between thirty thousand and the principal on that forty-eight thousand. It's so blamed obvious there ought to be a catch in it."

"Yes," said Mosson, "and don't forget the catch in it. Two! Two with equal motives, time, and opportunity. Damn it."

"I can't believe it," said Redfield, "and I won't. There's a loophole, a big loophole."

"Not such a very big loophole, Redfield," said Mosson.

"I'm thinking of possibilities; your point of view isn't mine, Mosson, it can't be. To me it's more possible that an outsider got in than that one of those children did this."

"Well, let's tackle it," said Griggs. "What kind of an outsider? A mighty smart one—no lunatic. You say your aunt was getting queer, Mr. Redfield. How queer? Flighty enough to make a lot of enemies without caring what happened afterwards?"

Redfield turned his eyes on Gamadge. "What do you think, Gamadge?"

"The impression she conveyed," said Gamadge, "was one of extreme flightiness."

"Did it reach irresponsibility?" asked Mosson.

"It seemed to. Definitely."

"Well, I don't know." Redfield's hands were
clasped behind his head, and his eyes were fixed on
the ceiling. "She seemed shrewd enough when it was
a matter of business. She wasn't irresponsible there.
But of course she hadn't much time lately for problems on the earthly plane. First she was wrapped up
in the study of the stars, and then she took up this
preposterous sun cult; which was her own invention,
if you ask me. One humored her, but it was something of a worry. This last companion she had—this
Miss Gouch—excellent creature, sensible, not young
herself; she knew how to manage Aunt, or at least, I
thought she did. But lately Miss Gouch began to
worry about the sun cult, and in fact she badgered
me about it. Aunt would talk, you know, about being
absorbed in the System. Whatever that meant. But
Gouch worried. Well, it *might* have ended in
suicide—"

"Suicide?" Griggs was alert.

"But I never thought so. All nonsense. I told
Gouch last spring not to fuss about it; told her to let
Aunt go her own way and pay no attention. So far as
I could see, Aunt adored life. What do you think, Ga-
madge?"

"Savored it, yes."

"But Gouch didn't like the responsibility, especially
as she was down for something in Aunt's will, and
was afraid of being blamed if anything happened.
Was, I say. Not any more! Aunt was very touchy
about her spiritual life. Wouldn't stand interference
in that department. Gouch was a fool; she interfered,
and Aunt turned her off and cut her out of her will
and made the new one."

"Oh dear," said Mosson.

"I was horrified, and if I only knew where the woman was I'd send her an honorarium myself. Aunt worked her like a horse, she was doing all the housekeeping since the servant shortage. And, if you please, Aunt made her stay on and close the Pasadena house and see her off on the train! They parted at the Los Angeles station, and nobody knows where she went to, and now I never shall know."

Griggs spoke slowly, after a pause: "Your aunt didn't leave any memorandum of her home address? This Miss Gouch's home address? There's no way we could find out—"

"I don't think so. Aunt said Gouch had insulted her most sacred feelings, and that so far as Aunt was concerned Gouch didn't exist any more."

Mosson looked at Griggs, eyebrows lifting. "The loophole?"

Griggs shuffled his papers. "Well . . . these elderly women—you don't know what they'll do if they've brooded long enough over a thing. How much was she down for in your aunt's will, Mr. Redfield?"

"Quite a lot; little annuity of I think five hundred per annum."

"That was a disappointment. She knew about it, you say?"

"I certainly meant to imply that she did."

Griggs himself brooded now: "Gouch knew Mrs. Malcolm was coming here, probably worked out the trip for her. Followed along, perhaps got into the grounds more than once this summer."

"Pleasant thought." Redfield closed his eyes to shut it out.

"Came along today by bus," continued Griggs. "Sunday—big crowds, buses jammed. She'd plan for that. Walked in and went down to the garden this afternoon, hung around in the woods behind the rose garden, heard the talk about the rifle. Saw Miss Malcolm go up to the tool house, saw pretty much where the rest of the party was. Dodged into the enclosure, watched Gamadge and Mrs. Malcolm go up to the rockery. Nothing to it. Afterwards she ran up through the woods again and out."

Redfield said: "It sounds most improbable to me, but if it's even the barest possibility, let's hang on to it for dear life."

"What was she like, Mr. Redfield?" Griggs took up his pen.

"Oh Lord, how do I know? I hardly saw the woman while I was with Aunt; she didn't even sit at meals with us. Aunt wouldn't have considered that at all fair to me. Let's see: she was going gray, I know that. Medium height, thin features, looked intelligent and even good-natured. If she's a murderer," said Redfield, "she didn't look like one when I last had the pleasure of seeing her."

"Color of eyes?" Griggs was writing busily.

"Vaguely blue or gray. Competent but fussy; I thought she fussed a little too much over Aunt Josephine; elderly ladies hate to be treated as if they were decrepit. But Lord, angels couldn't please 'em."

Mosson asked: "Was that thing down in the garden really part of her religion, or was it only a kind of emblem or reminder?"

"I don't quite know what it meant to her. It was a foolish thing for me to collect, but it amused me—part of that old circus! I suppose I saw the last of those when I was a boy. Or do they still come to Rivertown, Mosson?"

"No. I don't know whether there are any more of the little one-ring shows left in these parts."

"Well, it seemed to me a pleasing relic of rural gaiety. But when she saw it in the lumber room—I must confess she seemed to take it a trifle more seriously than was quite sensible. I humored her"—he smiled faintly—"you all know why, now—when she wanted it in the garden. But although I wouldn't admit it before, it really did rather get on my nerves. What do you think, Gamadge? *Was* she taking it seriously?"

"I couldn't quite make out," said Gamadge. "I couldn't quite make *her* out. I made a foolish joke about sunstroke, and she seemed to pity me more than she resented my flippancy. Perhaps she'd resent skepticism from a lady-companion more than from a man and a recent acquaintance."

Griggs tapped the table with his pen. "I suppose," he said, "that we ought to check up on her; unless . . ."

"Unless we get something definite nearer home. Thin stuff, the Gouch stuff," said Mosson. "And hard to check, too. Who's to remember her in the Los Angeles station? In these times? Perhaps through her trunk—"

"If she had a trunk," growled Lieutenant Griggs.

"I seem to see a collection of superannuated hold-alls," murmured Redfield.

"Especially in these times," repeated Mosson. "Well, it would be a long search and an expensive one. We might advertise. We might inquire at Rivertown and Old Bridge bus station. But why not concentrate now on what's under our noses? I know how you feel about it, Redfield; but we have no prejudice in favor of the two persons who benefit hugely by your aunt's death."

"And they had that feeling against her," said Griggs, "on account of the mother."

"I never told you they had feeling," protested Redfield. "I only gave you the bare facts of their lives. You're going on inference. I knew you would!"

"Well, Redfield," said Mosson, smiling at him, "wouldn't you?"

"They're good children," said Redfield, his eyes tightly shut again. "Lots of children won't make friends with a stepmother. But now it was going to be all right; and they knew years ago that Aunt wanted them to have two thousand apiece from her a year. They agreed to meet her. I arranged it. It's all my fault."

Griggs shuffled his notes. Then he cleared his throat, and said briskly: "I'll get hold of the officer that takes shorthand. We'll have the servants in first, and then Miss Ryder. Clear them out of the way. We know already that the cook and the maids were together, and that they didn't see any strangers. And we know what Miss Ryder knows. I'll just get it on the record."

Johnny swung his legs to the floor and got up. "Then I'll clear out. You won't want me here."

"No. Thanks, Mr. Redfield."

"I'll be in my sitting room upstairs, or next door in the living room, or in the dining room later."

"Shall I go?" asked Gamadge, as Redfield went out and closed the door.

"Like to have you here," said Griggs. He looked at Mosson. "All right with you, Mr. Mosson?"

"All right with me."

Griggs went out, leaving the door open. Malcolm's voice came to them from the living room.

"And you'll see the nice modern villa or château," he was saying, "and right in the side yard the ruins of the old dungeon and the tower. The air should be heavy with cliché; but is it? No! Not one platitude ever soils the lips of those French. They . . ."

Griggs came back, followed by a state policeman who carried a notebook.

"Just sit over there, Ames," he said, "by the lamp. And pull up three chairs in front of this table. There are three maids, two colored." He looked at Gamadge. "Doesn't the white maid mind?"

"Oh, no," said Gamadge. "Tilly Wirtz thinks that the Debenhams are very distinguished."

7

Feudal

"Distinguished, are they?" Mosson, who was freshening his highball, looked amused.

"Very. The cook—Reina—is the best type of West Indian, brought up in the British colonial tradition. Redfield calls her Debby. Her daughter Alice is American born and bred; she's had two years of college, and wouldn't be doing housework here if Debby didn't need her. Tilly Wirtz is Austrian, from somewhere near Salzburg; limpidly honest, awfully stupid, getting on in years. Redfield picked her up in a hotel over there, and got her to this country years ago. But she hasn't made much sense of us yet, and doesn't speak English very well."

The studio door opened, and a small procession entered. It was headed by a tall and large black woman, who wore a white uniform. A magenta handkerchief was tied about her head, and there were handsome gold hoops in her ears. She looked grave, aloof, and calm.

Alice, a mere wisp beside her mother, came next. Tilly Wirtz brought up the rear—a small, pale-haired creature in spectacles, whose skirts reached her black-clad ankles. She had a meek, innocent, confiding look, but it was plain that policemen filled her with a great awe.

"Now just sit down in those chairs," said Griggs, in a benevolent voice, "where I can talk to you. That's right. Don't be nervous; we know you had nothing to do with what happened this afternoon. You were all in sight of each other, clearing off the cocktail party and organizing dinner."

Debby, who looked anything but nervous, said: "About dinner, sir. Mr. Redfield has ordered a buffet supper instead in the dining room. It's ready now. Everybody's to go and eat in there, and so are the officers and the gentlemen down in the garden."

"That's like Redfield," observed Mosson.

"Yes, sir. But Mr. Redfield wants to know if you gentlemen want trays in here."

"Mr. Mosson and I do," said Griggs. "We'll let you know when. Now what we want to know from you three is this: Would it be easy for strangers to get into the place any time during the day? Any day?"

After a pause for reflection, Debby said: "Strangers don't come way out here, Lieutenant; but they could get in. You know Alice and I have our apartment in the cottage across the drive?"

"Yes."

"Well, we don't go back and forth much in a day; not unless we have some special errand like changing our uniforms for the afternoon. We have a sitting room over here, too. We have a radio in it. It looks out on the terrace, and the kitchen and pantry windows are high."

"Miss Wirtz."

Tilly, who seemed to have something on her mind, started. She looked at Griggs vacantly.

"You have your room in the house here, Miss Wirtz?"

"Upstairs at de end of de north wing, and a nice bath."

"You don't sit up there in the daytime and look out of your windows?"

Tilly seemed shocked at this. "If I have time off I sit in our sitting room and listen to de music."

Reina said: "I wish some stranger did get in today, sir. To take the blame off the house. It was an accident, but even so I wish you could find some stranger to take the blame off the house."

"If it was an accident," said Griggs dryly, "nobody's owned up."

"Ladies and gentlemen often have accidents with guns in the Islands."

"Ladies and gentlemen," retorted Griggs, "own up."

"Yes, sir; in the Islands."

"Anywhere," snapped Griggs. "Forget whether it was an accident, and just remember that anyhow this unfortunate lady was shot dead."

The three seemed to reflect on the fact, but without grief.

"And we have to find out how it happened," continued Griggs, "no matter who gets the blame."

Debby turned her majestic head and looked at Tilly Wirtz. Tilly, avoiding her eye, gazed at the wall above Griggs' head. Debby turned again to face him.

"Of course," she said, "I'm always in my kitchen when I'm not in our sitting room or in our apartment across the drive. I don't see the guests that come here, and I never go upstairs. But I told Alice and Tilly that it's their duty to do what they can to help you, just as if they'd taken their solemn oath in a court of justice."

Gamadge, looking at the faces of his colleagues, and seeing nothing there but gratification, interposed: "You haven't taken a solemn oath, Debby; and this isn't a court of justice. You don't any of you have to say a thing, but if you do it ought to be the truth. That's all."

Debby turned towards him, raised her head so that she seemed to be looking down at him from an immense height of conscious rectitude, and replied in her deep, melodious voice:

"Morally, Mr. Gamadge, it's as if we were bound by our solemn oaths in a court of justice."

"And that," said Mosson to Gamadge in a thin whisper, "fixes *you*."

The severe countenance of Griggs had relaxed into an expression of pleased interest: "They want to make a statement, Mrs. Debenham?"

"Tilly does. All *I* know," said Debby, "is that Mrs. Malcolm was crazy. I hardly ever saw her. But if a colored person put up a thing in his garden in the Islands—a thing like that thing Mrs. Malcolm made Mr. Redfield put up in the rose garden—the Governor would send to ask why."

Griggs sat back to digest this if possible. "It's only a figure off a circus wagon."

"That lady," said Mrs. Debenham, "didn't want it there because it was off a circus wagon. Mr. Redfield did; or anyway, he thought of putting it up in the kitchen garden for fun. But Mrs. Malcolm . . . She wasn't in my kitchen three times all summer, but when she did come, something bad came with her."

Alice, showing mortification, protested: "She was

just eccentric, Mother. There wasn't anything wrong
about Mrs. Malcolm. She was pleasant enough. And
that wooden image—you know people like Mr. Redfield's friends have their own kind of fun. It was just
her fun, putting it in the rose garden. You sound so
old-fashioned, Mother, when you talk like that."

"Well," said Debby, without looking at her, "I
didn't say she died of magic. Tilly—remember what
we said."

Tilly Wirtz, without other warning than the extrac-
tion of a pink handkerchief from her apron pocket,
burst into loud sobs.

"Tilly," said Mrs. Debenham, looking straight in
front of her, "it wouldn't be right to keep it to yourself."

"Certainly wouldn't," agreed Griggs.

Tilly sobbed.

"Come on," said Griggs, "what was it?"

Tilly put away her handkerchief. "I wish I hadn't
told Reina and Alice. De young chentleman was
choking."

"Choking?"

"Chust choking wit his sister."

"What were they joking about?"

Tilly insisted on explaining the circumstances first;
how she had come to overhear them.

Immediately after the twins' arrival, and their in-
troduction to the deceased, they had gone up to the
rooms they always occupied when they came to Idlers.
The rooms, a guest suite with a bath between, extended along the north wing. Beyond them was a series of
cupboards, and then came Tilly's room and a servants' bath, at the head of the back stairs.

David Malcolm had the end room, and Tilly, not

knowing that he had come upstairs, arrived at its half-open door with towels for the communicating bath. She could get into the bath only through one bedroom or the other.

She had been arrested on his threshold by the sound of his voice.

"He said," she quavered, " 'Dis is our big chance, Cora. But which of us will bump her off?' "

"Bump her off," repeated Griggs, dreamily.

"It means—*keel* somebody!"

"So it does."

"But he was choking. Miss Malcolm was standing I tink in de bathroom doorway. I didn't hear what she said. He said: 'She's worse dan we expected. How about using an ax?' And Miss Malcolm said: 'Sh. You want to ruin us?' And I came away."

Griggs sat looking at her. After a pause he said as if to himself: "They weren't here much. They may have thought you were *all* in that cottage across the drive."

"A French gentleman might think so," said Mrs. Debenham, dryly. "And Mr. Malcolm is practically French."

"You repeated all this to the others?" Griggs turned back to Tilly.

She had done so, thinking it was rather a joke herself—on Mrs. Malcolm, whom nobody seemed much to care for. When, said Tilly, Mrs. Malcolm was in fact bumped off, the three had consulted again. They were all aware—Alice had heard plenty of talk in the living room and dining room—of the twins' financial position and expectations.

Mosson cleared his throat. "Miss Wirtz: were names mentioned? I mean could you swear Mr. Malcolm and his sister were talking about their stepmother?"

Tilly, suddenly producing the pink handkerchief again, said that the name "Mrs. Malcolm" had been pronounced by the young man.

"And anyhow," said Alice, in her quiet voice, "he couldn't have been talking about Mrs. Drummond, because he knew Mrs. Drummond already."

Griggs stared. "Why should he have meant Mrs. Drummond? You mean he might have meant Mrs. Drummond if he and Miss Malcolm hadn't met her already?"

"Just in joke. She was annoying him so last summer."

Griggs looking bemused at this, as indeed Mosson did also, she went on in an expository tone: "This is the third year they've been coming, you know. They came first in the fall of nineteen forty. They've known Mr. and Mrs. Drummond three years."

"I know; but how was Mrs. Drummond annoying him?" Griggs, apparently rather annoyed himself, repeated the question in a different form: "How should Mrs. Drummond annoy anybody?"

"Well, running after him," said Alice carelessly. "They were great friends at first, but last summer, and this summer before Mrs. Malcolm came, she ran after him. It embarrassed Mr. Redfield, I think. And I do think that Mr. Malcolm joked about it a little with his sister; in a nice way, you know."

Her words had fallen into a dead silence. In a dead silence she began again: "I don't think Mr. Redfield would have asked the Drummonds over today, but he's so sorry for them now. They used to be so rich, and now they're so poor with the taxes."

After another period of silence, Mosson asked in a

tone of mild interest: "How did Mr. Drummond take it?"

Alice needed no gloss on this question: "I don't think he paid any attention. He's such great friends with Miss Malcolm." She added: "I don't mean anything serious; it's just their kind of fun, you know."

The next half minute was punctuated every few seconds by Tilly's catches of breath. But Tilly didn't look interested. Perhaps her capacity for interest in such matters had been exhausted in European hotels.

At last Griggs said: "That all? Thanks. Fine. You understand that at the inquest tomorrow all you'll have to do will be to answer questions? It'll be purely formal tomorrow. Just answer questions."

He saw them out of the studio, closed the door, and came back to sink into his chair. "Great heck, they'd—I must warn the M. E."

Mosson's head was back against his cushions. "We're all living on a volcano," he said in a sepulchral voice.

"No," remarked Gamadge, "not all of us. Johnny wasn't blown up. Surely you realize that they were only 'taking the blame off the house'? They're protecting Redfield. They're feudal."

"Redfield would hate this. He certainly didn't inspire it—to my own knowledge he hasn't exchanged a syllable with those servants since the murder. He sent them instructions about the buffet supper through that officer out there—Stromer. Miss Ryder told me everything he did before that—she was with him. My God, that girl—Alice—she's trying to suggest that the Drummonds had a motive for the murder."

"I got it," said Griggs. "Hinting they had an interest in the Malcolm twins getting the money. Would you think a girl like that Alice would have the brains?"

Gamadge said: "She's above small gossip, and so is her mother, and Tilly hasn't an ounce of malice in her. They simply don't intend Redfield to be involved. He's the kind of employer who deserves loyalty."

"He'd be wild," said Mosson. "Mrs. Drummond! Who'd have thought it?" He groaned faintly. "What a murder case brings out!"

"Mrs. Drummond isn't much of a mixer," said Griggs, "but she isn't unpopular. Drummond's liked. We'll have to go easy on this."

"I can't get over the subtlety of that Debenham girl's attack," said Mosson.

Ames, the officer who was acting as stenographer, looked up from his notes. He said: "I've seen Mr. Drummond and Miss Malcolm once or twice walking on the back roads."

"That stuff may not be left on the record at all," Griggs warned him. "Look out with it." He rose. "Well, I'll get Miss Ryder. Perhaps another miracle will happen, and I'll get something from her."

"Don't get your hopes up," said Gamadge. "She's feudal too; but her loyalty is to a code."

"Miss Ryder wouldn't lie to us."

"No, but she won't give you impressions for facts. She'll hand you those, if she has any. She would take a thing of this kind, and her obligations to the law, very seriously."

"That's something." He opened the door, put his head into the living room, and said: "If you please, Miss Ryder."

Self-reliant and disciplined of spirit, always calm in

a crisis, she was composed enough now; but it was ev-
ident that she was deeply shocked and distressed. She
said: "How do you do, Mr. Mosson," glanced at Ames
in his corner, and made for the row of chairs in front
of Griggs' table. "Am I to sit here?"

"Sit any place you want to, Miss Ryder."

"If the others sat here, I will."

Gamadge said, as he and the other men resumed
their seats, "The lieutenant means that you're only a
witness, Abby, not a suspect."

"I hope he doesn't think Alice and Reina and Tilly
Wirtz are suspects?"

"No, but they wouldn't have taken the occasion
seriously if he hadn't put them in a row."

She said: "I suppose it was very lucky for me that I
picked this spray," and looked down at it; it was in
the buttonhole of her gray jacket, and Gamadge
thought how like her it was to have preserved it. He
couldn't imagine Abigail picking a thing and then
throwing it away. She respected the lives of plants
and flowers.

"I'd like to say, Lieutenant Griggs," she began,
"and Mr. Mosson too, if he had anything to do with
it, that I think it was kind to let Johnny keep poor
Mrs. Malcolm's body here until the funeral."

"We were consulting our own convenience, I'm
afraid, Miss Ryder," said Mosson. "This studio is a
good place to hold an inquest in, you know, and the
house is central. Right in the middle of the county."

"Well, I'm glad he could keep her here. It's a
dreadful thing for Johnny Redfield."

Mosson said: "I gather that you're inclined to wipe
him off the list, then."

"The list?"

"Of possible murderers."

"There are no possible murderers on my list of acquaintances."

"That's definite, anyhow. Mr. Redfield tells us he had a financial motive; his aunt's property, about thirty thousand dollars."

"I shouldn't murder anybody for thirty thousand dollars; I don't know why I should think other people would. Other sane people, I mean. Other decent people. Lieutenant Griggs—"

"Yes, Miss Ryder?"

"Could some insane person have got in?"

"Well . . ." Griggs pursed up his lips. "I suppose anybody could have got in. But an insane person? There were those gloves, you know, and that piled-up turf. It wasn't insane to use all those precautions."

"But there are monomaniacs who are very cunning."

Griggs said: "We'll keep the possibility in mind." He shuffled his papers, and then looked up at her: "You've had your place here a long time, haven't you, Miss Ryder?"

"Oh goodness, yes. We had a lot of property in this part of the world once."

"Ryders, Redfields, Drummonds. They go 'way back."

"But I sold everything off long ago, luckily for me. Everything but my few acres down the hill. We all had real farms once; my grandmother took charge in her own dairy. I had my own little churn, and I always went up to the pastures in the evening to help round up the cows. I had a calf given me every summer, and I never could see why it had vanished the next year."

"You've known the Drummonds all your life, haven't you?"

"I've known Walter all *his* life. I've known Blanche since he married her, a dozen years ago."

"Would you object to saying whether you know of any kind of a love affair between Mrs. Drummond and Mr. David Malcolm?"

She looked less angry than disturbed. After a moment she said: "I suppose you have to ask all kinds of questions, but I don't know why you should ask that. And I can't answer you, because I don't know a thing about it. I shouldn't dream of gossiping to the police." She added severely: "I hope you aren't being led astray. Mr. Malcolm is a very interesting young man, and we're all fond of him." After another pause she amplified this: "The Drummonds and the Malcolms have a great deal in common—they're all good at sports."

"I understand that Miss Malcolm and Drummond are great friends," said Griggs, studying his notes.

Abigail was silent. Presently she said: "I suppose it's those silly maids. I hope it isn't Henry Gamadge. If it is"—she cast a withering look at him—"all I can say is that criminology has ruined his character."

"Gamadge hasn't said a word," declared Mosson.

"People put such horrible constructions on the simplest and most harmless behavior," said Abigail.

"So they do." Griggs looked up at her. "The deceased, now. Redfield's cook thinks she was definitely crazy. Some kind of a witch or something, too."

"I must say I thought better of Reina Debenham. Mrs. Malcolm was flighty and odd. That's all."

"Was she the kind to make enemies, would you say?"

"I don't really know. I only met her twice. Enemies?" Miss Ryder pondered. "She certainly wasn't tactful." Then she cast a hasty glance at Gamadge, who was looking at the fire, and added: "But people aren't murdered for tactlessness, fortunately for us all."

"Wonder why the servants disliked her so much."

"Johnny Redfield did say that she gave a good deal of trouble; required waiting on, and didn't like Reina's coffee, which is delicious but a trifle more roasted than we get it. Reina roasted it herself, when she could get the beans."

"Did Mrs. Malcolm talk to you about that companion of hers, that Miss Gouch?"

"I think she did, once, last July. In the course of conversation."

"Did you get any impression that there was ill feeling there? Mr. Redfield seemed to think that Miss Gouch was treated rather shabbily by Mrs. Malcolm because she insulted her religion—that sun cult, you know, or whatever it was."

"Religion?" Miss Ryder looked aloof and vague. "Would you call it a religion? I'm Anglican-Catholic myself, and rather high."

Mosson interposed gravely: "You evidently didn't have much in common with the deceased, Miss Ryder."

"Nothing at all," said Abigail cheerfully, "so far as tastes go."

"She didn't talk about this Miss Gouch in a way that made you think Miss Gouch was an enemy?" asked Griggs.

"No," said Abigail, rather startled. "She didn't at

all. She was rather complimentary about her, as I remember the conversation."

"Now these young Malcolms."

"Lieutenant," said Abigail, "I cannot believe that either of them would commit a crime. I don't know them well, of course; I've barely met them. I haven't exchanged twenty words with either of them since they first began coming up here to stay with Johnny Redfield. But they're both highly educated and well-bred, and such people simply do not murder people all of a sudden. They can't. It isn't possible."

"Not all of a sudden, no."

"If you're thinking about the way they felt towards their stepmother, then I can only say that millions of people feel like that, and don't commit murder."

"I wasn't thinking about the way they felt towards their stepmother, Miss Ryder."

"You're thinking about the money."

"Yes. That's the big motive for murder."

"Well, all I can say is that two people who behaved less as though they meant to commit a murder . . ."

"Can't go by that, can we?"

"Of course, Miss Ryder," said Mosson, "we can't expect you to look at these things as we professionals do. But you suggest an insane criminal; I suggest—off the record—that a young person with a grudge can nurse that grudge until there's nothing else left for him in life. Or for her. I can think of two feminine examples, and one of them was only sixteen. And both were members of the upper-middle-class, and to this day a lot of people—in spite of the sixteen-year-old's confession—can't believe she did it. Here we have a big stake in money besides the other motive; I shouldn't be at all surprised to find that something very like insanity might have developed. Hasn't this young Malcolm a head injury that never got well?"

Abigail, looking deeply depressed, said that he had. "But don't call *him* insane, Mr. Mosson! You ought to hear him talk. He's as cool and chatty as if—as if nothing had happened."

"In his present circumstances," said Mosson, "I'm not sure that it's particularly sane of him to be cool and chatty."

Griggs rose, and the others also got to their feet. Griggs said: "You can go home whenever you want to, Miss Ryder. Thanks for giving us your opinion."

"I'll wait and see whether I can be of any further use to Johnny Redfield." She stood looking from one to the other representative of authority. "You couldn't use any of this guesswork as evidence, could you?"

"Afraid we couldn't," said Mosson. "We're just trying to get a picture."

He opened the door for her. When he turned back he was smiling. So was Griggs.

"Go ahead and gloat," said Gamadge. "Poor Abby."

"I said Miss Ryder wouldn't lie," Griggs reminded him smugly.

"What I call transparent honesty," agreed Mosson. "You can see right through it. I don't think she includes Cora Malcolm in the case, though; she didn't bother to give her a build-up."

"Well"—Griggs started for the door—"we'll clear off the Drummonds now. Start with Mrs."

Mosson sank back upon his sofa. He said gloomily: "I hate this case."

"So do I," said Griggs. "Hate it like poison."

8

Animated

State Officer Stromer, who ushered Blanche Drummond into the studio, was a phlegmatic youth; but even he stood for a moment as if bedazzzled, looking after the straight, tall, long-waisted figure, and the curled arrangement of gold-brown hair drawn up from the long white neck, before he withdrew and shut the vision out.

It was the new animation in her face that made it seem really beautiful, the unwonted color in her cheeks that brightened her eyes. But the brightness made the eyes seem harder, and the animation aged her by years. Gamadge had never seen her so handsome or so old.

She went quickly around the end of Mosson's sofa and sat down beside him.

"Mr. Mosson," she said, "isn't this dreadful? Could you give me a drink? I really need one."

Mosson began to pour the drink. Griggs, ignored and rather at a loss, waited standing behind his table. Gamadge, ignored, leaned forward smiling to push the siphon nearer and drop a piece of ice in her tumbler.

"Walter and I were so glad to know you were here," said Blanche. "It's such a comfort to have somebody on the spot who knows all about such things and isn't likely to jump to conclusions. Now of course we all think that an insane person got in. Unless that little Wilson boy—"

Mosson said: "Here's your highball, Mrs. Drummond. The Wilson boy was at home with his family. I wonder if you'd be so good as to address yourself to Lieutenant Griggs? He's conducting the examination of witnesses."

"Oh." Her head slowly turned, and she smiled at Griggs. "How silly of me. Am I to sit there?" She rose, glass in hand. "I didn't know this was a formal investigation. I thought the sheriff conducted them— our dear old sheriff in Old Bridge."

Gamadge, with a knowing grin at her, carried his little table over and set it beside the middle witness chair.

"Less than dust though I be," he murmured, "let me make myself useful in my poor way."

"Henry, darling, we adore you! But you're not a professional. We must rely on professionals now." She sat down, took a cigarette from Gamadge, and a light.

Griggs sat glumly down and looked at her. "Sheriff is on holiday," he said. "And we're out of the town limits anyway. We scratched up a deputy in Old Bridge, though, and he's now down in the grounds helping our cameraman. You won't get anything more formal than this, Mrs. Drummond, until the inquest tomorrow afternoon."

"Oh. I see." She sat with her tumbler in one hand, her cigarette drooping from the fingers of the other. Her long, slim legs were extended, her feet crossed. Officer Ames dragged his eyes from the shimmering convolutions of her hair and applied himself to his notes.

"Now I understand," said Griggs, "that this afternoon you caught up with Mr. David Malcolm outside that rose garden—while he was hanging up a couple of dead crows—and had a word with him."

"Oh; yes. I did. But I didn't catch up with him, exactly, you know!" She made the correction with gentle tolerance. "I just happened to pass him; I was on my way to the greenhouse."

"Would you tell me what he said to you?"

"What he said to me? Why on earth do you—but of course you must have some reason for asking that. Let me see. There had been some talk about our going down for a walk to the swimming pool, but I had realized that it would be rough and perhaps wet, and"—she looked at her delicate shoes—"I decided not to go. I told him I wasn't going after all, and I think he just said all right."

"And he went off alone?"

"Well, I didn't see him go, because I walked straight across the road and over to the greenhouse."

"You stayed inside there for fifteen minutes or more, probably twenty," said Griggs.

"Did I?" She took a sip of highball. "To tell you the truth, Lieutenant," she smiled at him, "I was a little tired of the party. I had had quite enough of poor Mrs. Malcolm. She embarrassed me."

"Embarrassed you?"

"Her clothes were so insane. She wore a wreath, you know, poor old soul, and a sort of dressing gown, and bare feet in beach sandals. To be perfectly frank, it made me sick to look at her."

Griggs picked up a sheet of paper and put it down

again. "You were just killing time in that green-house?"

"Until I could decently suggest going home."

"You heard that third shot—the one that killed Mrs. Malcolm?"

"Yes, I did; faintly."

"Who did you think fired it?"

"I didn't think. I knew the rifle was there where David Malcolm left it, and I didn't know that Henry Gamadge and Mrs. Malcolm had left the place. I thought—or rather I should have thought if I'd thought anything—that Henry had fired it." She added: "Of course people will say that the Malcolms had a motive."

"People?"

"People that don't know them."

"They had a motive, Mrs. Drummond."

"But they didn't know they'd have an opportunity. They didn't know Mrs. Malcolm was going up to the rockery, and they didn't know they could shoot her from that one place in the rose garden." She added brightly: "I don't know what you can do in a case like this."

Griggs looked at her.

"I mean you can't arrest both the Malcolms, can you, just because one of them might have done it?"

Griggs said after a pause: "This is a preliminary examination. The evidence hasn't more than begun to come in yet. And you mustn't assume that we're only thinking of the Malcolms, Mrs. Drummond."

"But who on earth else . . ." She stared at him. Then she said: "I meant that you simply have to have something definite, before you arrest people. Don't you?"

"Definite? Motive's definite, Mrs. Drummond."

"But don't juries want *more,* when they're—oh, it's too ridiculous! The Malcolms! If you only knew them! That is, nobody *can* know Cora; but at least they'd know she wouldn't commit a murder. David is the simplest, kindest—why, he's a perfect child. And he was ever so much farther away from the place than Cora was—he picked those asters by the pool. That's twice as far as the tool house."

"You know Mr. Malcolm pretty well, Mrs. Drummond? You sound as though you did."

Her color heightened. "We all try to do what we can for him. He needs amusement. He's been through so much. Didn't you know?"

"I heard something. Well, you don't seem to have information that's likely to be of use to us. You didn't see a soul going through that wicket gate or coming out of it after you came out of it yourself. That right?"

"Yes."

"That'll be all for now."

She got up, stood there a moment as if trying to make up her mind to say something more, and then walked slowly across the studio to the door. Mosson held it for her.

"Well," he said, returning to his seat, "she had a little fun with you at first, Griggs. I hope she isn't disappointed in the professionals."

"She ought to trust us to remember Miss Malcolm," said Griggs. "That was a raw steer."

"I must say I shouldn't have thought she could work out the thing as well as she did."

"I bet she'd have Malcolm," said Griggs, "whether he'd done it or not. She's in love with him, all right.

Ten years younger, is he? That makes it worse. She wouldn't tell us if she'd seen him go in there and come out on the dead run."

"Who would tell us what?" asked Mosson. "Would Drummond give her away? Or give Miss Malcolm away? Would the Malcolms give each other or the Drummonds away? Would Redfield give any of them away? Oh, how I hate this case."

"And if it was both the Malcolms," said Griggs, "how do we show collusion?"

"And if anybody else tells us that it was an insane person from somewhere," said Mosson, "I'll certainly show temper. Why didn't you keep on at her about Malcolm, Griggs? Here Alice the maid gives you a nice tip, and you don't take it."

Griggs said angrily: "All the evidence points to Malcolm being tired of Mrs. Drummond. Why should she kill his stepmother so he'd get the money, and divorce his wife, and marry *her*—after she'd divorced Drummond—if he's tired of her?"

"I'm surprised at you. Malcolm pretends to be tired of her so that when she does commit the murder they won't be suspected of conspiracy." Mosson turned his cynical smile upon Gamadge, who had resumed his seat and was looking at the fire. "What do you say to that, Gamadge?"

"Don't ask me questions yet," said Gamadge, without moving. "I'm trying to adjust my mind to all this. I'm trying to make myself believe that one of these people may be a murderer. It's not so easy, you know. I didn't imagine it this afternoon, when I allowed the deceased to stand up against a tree and wait to be shot at. And yet I knew the obvious motive for the murder then, and could have guessed at less obvious ones; I knew the gun was there, loaded. There was ill feeling in the air, plenty of it, too. But I didn't feel murder in the air, Mosson."

"It doesn't as a rule advertise itself," said Mosson, looking ironically at him.

"Well, it often does."

"We'll have Drummond in." Griggs went over to the door, opened it a crack, barked: "Mr. Drummond!" and waited. If he feared that remarks from the studio might seep out among the occupants of the living room he need have been under no such apprehension. Gamadge and Mosson waited in silence.

Walter Drummond came in with long, lurching strides, stopped, and looked at Officer Ames, at Gamadge, and at Mosson. Gamadge returned the look with a new interest. Drummond's sunburn was the kind that repeats itself at every weekend; peels, and blisters. His nose was peeling now, but in spite of the disfigurement Gamadge realized that he was a very good-looking man. But his clipped moustache concealed the length of a long and obstinate upper lip, which looked more than ever obstinate now.

He said rather loudly: "The party needn't have been inside the rose garden at all; might have stood at the corner outside and then thrown the gloves and rifle over the trellis. Those squares of turf—Johnny doesn't remember anything about them. That woman—the dead woman—just crazy enough to go down there and dig them herself. Nobody could follow *her* line of thought. I mean, it's unfair to assume that the gun was fired by a small person trying to make it look as though it might have been a taller person. It isn't fair."

Gamadge had never seen him so eager.

"Well, Mr. Drummond," said Griggs, "it would have been a big risk. Won't you sit down?"

Drummond looked about him vaguely, and then came forward and sat in the middle chair in front of the table. He said: "It was an outside job, and the party was insane."

Lieutenant Griggs and Gamadge shot a quick look at the State's Attorney; but Mosson restrained himself from unprofessional behavior. He merely put his fingertips together, and looked at Drummond with a faint smile.

Drummond's large and square hands clasped the arms of his chair. He sat forward, as if he might at any moment spring up again. How old was he? Forty or more? He went on talking:

"The woman was daft. How do we know what enemies she had? I mean you can't go by guesswork. Any good lawyer—"

"We haven't got as far as the trial yet, Mr. Drummond," said Griggs. "Or as far as lawyers; unless you want one."

"I don't want a lawyer."

"You'll tell us what you did this afternoon, from the time you left the house with Miss Malcolm?"

"Certainly. We went straight down to the flower garden."

"You didn't care to watch your wife and Mr. Malcolm shoot crows?"

"No. We heard the shots. But Miss Malcolm didn't stay—she went off to see about her croquet game."

"You didn't care for that idea?"

"I'll explain." Drummond's hands slid back and forth along the arms of his chair. "I was going to cut flowers for Redfield. The thing is, we've been neighbors—his family and mine have—for generations. Good neighbors, you know. Obliged each other with produce and so on when needed. We always made a point of swapping stuff in season—and flowers. Perhaps you know what flowers mean in the country? In these old houses?"

Griggs making no reply, he went on:

"Redfield sent snapdragon and things over to us earlier in the season, picked it himself. We were going to reciprocate with dahlias and zinnias, we thought it was going to be a good crop. But they didn't pan out to much after all, and the frost finished them. So today I thought I could at least cut some of his own things for him, if there should happen to be any. The cosmos—I didn't care for the look of it. Ragged, fading. That stuff has to be fresh, and I never did think it was much in the house. Not showy enough. There aren't many flowers except roses that look like anything in a small vase, either; but those button chrysanthemums are useful anywhere."

Talkative, Drummond was; extraordinarily talkative for him.

Griggs listened to his horticultural information with patience. When he came to a stop, however, Griggs was tapping his papers with a knotty finger.

"You're not here much nowadays, Mr. Drummond, I think?"

"No, only weekends and holidays. The younger men in the office are overseas."

"You were down there in that garden from about five minutes past five until five thirty-five or more. That's a long time to spend picking a bunch of chrysanthemums."

"I wandered around, smoked a couple of cigarettes,

looked the place over. The way anybody does in a garden."

"Or a greenhouse."

Drummond gazed at him blankly.

"But the important point for us is that you happened to be behind that cosmos so often. You were there when your wife and Malcolm came through after they shot the crows. You were there when Malcolm went back on his way down to the swimming pool. You didn't see them, and they didn't see you."

"That's so."

"And you must have been there again later; since you don't volunteer any statement to the effect that Malcolm never passed through the place again. Such a statement would clear him."

Drummond, still gazing at Lieutenant Griggs, said: "I didn't see him. Naturally I'd clear him if I could."

"Naturally."

"You don't get the layout of the place. If I was at the far end of it with my back turned—looking at a border, and so on—I wouldn't see anybody. I wouldn't have to be behind the cosmos. I wouldn't hear anybody, either; those paths are all turfed. It's only a few yards—the trip from the gate to where you go down into the orchard."

Mosson said: "Too bad."

Drummond turned to look at him: "I don't think the boy did it."

"Any reason for thinking so?"

"He'd just been using the rifle. Wouldn't use it again to commit a murder; or anyhow, in his place I shouldn't have."

"But he's supposed to be such a clever young man; cleverer than you or I."

Drummond said nothing.

"He knew where the rifle was," continued Mosson. "He knew that Mrs. Malcolm was wandering around the place. He needn't have planned a shot through the vines; that was luck—seeing her at that spot in the rockery, with light coming down just there through the trees. He could have got her anywhere on the place, and at longer range. Gamadge couldn't have prevented it, or found him later. He'd have his line of retreat all ready. But he or somebody did fire from the rose garden—I'm sorry to reject your theory of the party standing where Gamadge *could* have seen him, outside the place. And if it was Malcolm—well, you'll forgive the suggestion; this is an investigation of a murder—perhaps he thought that his friend's husband and his sister's friend would swear he hadn't gone through the flower garden twice again."

Drummond, slowly turning dark red under his sunburn, uttered no word.

"And though you don't say he went through, you don't say he didn't; which cancels out," said Mosson, "and leaves us where we were."

Drummond spoke at last: "You're telling me I'm lying?"

"I'm giving you the lawyer's point of view. You should know it as well as I do."

"I don't know whether he went through or not. I don't think he did it," said Drummond.

"Let me offer you a theory of my own; it eliminates deliberate murder, and yet it keeps the party who fired the rifle inside that rose garden. I don't know what you'll think of the idea." Mosson put his fingertips together. "Suppose we imagine a person—young person, unstable temperament, somebody who didn't like Mrs. Malcolm, and—er—a moral coward. The young person comes into, or comes back into, the rose garden at approximately five twenty-five. Sees Gamadge and Mrs. Malcolm walking up to the rockery. Wanders over to that statue, or whatever it is, and picks up the rifle. Thinks of shooting another crow, wanders back to the archway, and dodges along to the right, watching Mrs. Malcolm through the vines. Sights her up there against the tree, and aims the rifle—as a child would, you know. Psychology comes into it. Well: a twig catches in the trigger, or somehow it goes off. Psychopathology now? I think the late Freud says there *are* no accidents.

"Bang! The woman's dead. The joker's life's ruined. Or is it? Perhaps not, if the gardener's gloves are put on and the rifle well rubbed off; if those sods are piled. It would take pluck to wait and do that, but it would have taken more pluck to own up."

Drummond said after a long silence: "I don't think that happened. I don't think the rifle was put through the vines at all. I say it was done from outside, by an outsider."

"All right, Mr. Drummond," said Griggs.

Drummond stood upright and went as if blindly out of the studio.

"No special animus against Malcolm, I should say," Griggs reflected aloud. He had closed the door, but stood beside it.

"Didn't like Mrs. Malcolm," said Mosson. "*Might* have had an understanding with Cora Malcolm, and done the job for her. But in that case, why is he so all-fired anxious to keep the shooting out of the rose garden?"

Nobody told him.

9

You Could Go Crazy

Cora Malcolm came into the room, quiet and grave. She walked directly over to the table behind which Griggs was standing with a solemn look on his face, and stood as if waiting for further orders; she did not seem to be aware of Mosson's presence, or of Gamadge's, until the latter introduced the State's Attorney and the lieutenant of state police. Then she nodded to them.

"Please sit here, Miss Malcolm," said Griggs, "so I can talk to you about this tragedy. Now let's see. You left this house this afternoon with Mr. Drummond. Where did you go?"

She was looking at him intently. "Down to the lower garden. I didn't stay, because Mr. Drummond only had his pocketknife; you can't cut flowers without a knife or clippers."

"Neither of you thought of that before you started?"

"No, for some reason we didn't. I think we were thinking more of its being a stroll."

"Mr. Drummond wasn't; he had a long story for us about owing Mr. Redfield snapdragons or something; I can't remember a quarter of it, but Officer Ames there took notes; he'll read them to you if you like."

"No, thanks. I meant that *I* was thinking of it as a stroll."

"Mr. Drummond seemed to want to put it over about getting flowers for Mr. Redfield; but perhaps that was because he spent such a long time down there, away from everybody, and wanted to account for it."

"It that was his explanation, it's the true one."

"We can absolutely depend on his word, can we?"

"Yes." She added: "At least *I* think so."

"Getting the flowers wasn't just an excuse given to get you off for a private talk?"

"No."

"It looks as if he asked you down for a private talk, and you ran out on him. Afterwards you both kept away from the party for half an hour; I don't know whether I'm imagining things, but it looks funny to me."

"Perhaps it was a funny thing for me to do; rather rude, in fact. I didn't notice that time was going." She added: "I really should have liked a game of croquet; I've played a good deal here. Mr. Redfield has had a very sporting course laid out in the orchard, and we have our local rules. And we play for money."

"But when you got up to the tool house and got as far as getting out a mallet, you forgot about the croquet and sat down on the steps?"

"I was rather worried about my stepmother."

Griggs looked sharply at her. "Worried?"

"I suppose you know that she said she meant to give us—meant to double the allowances we had from my father. We'd always refused the money before, but Mr. Redfield wanted us to take it; wanted us to meet her. This autumn, when we came back from the country, he wrote and said she was here, and wouldn't we take advantage of the opportunity and come up. We accepted."

"Why this time?"

"As you get older you want money more, I suppose. But we didn't like her." Cora glanced down at her left lapel, glanced away, and went on: "We disliked her very much. There was something very disagreeable about her, we thought, apart from her being so odd and strange. She seemed actually malicious. As if she meant to make us *pay* for the money, you know. I didn't blame her for resenting our past behavior, but why meet us at all, much less give us two thousand a year apiece, if she didn't mean to forget the past?"

Griggs, somewhat taken aback by all this candor, looked steadily at her; he said nothing.

"So when I got to the tool house," said Cora, "I sat down and wondered whether we could take the money after all. I was trying to make up my mind to tell my brother—to say I would refuse my share."

"Well," said Griggs, staring at her, "it doesn't make much difference now, does it, which way you finally decided to act?"

"No. We get all the money now," said Cora in a lifeless tone. "When Mr. Gamadge told us she'd been killed like that—I can't describe how it struck me. Like one of those dooms in the Greek tragedies; as if she deliberately *were* making us pay. But I soon realized that she wouldn't choose that means! And I realized that David's motive and mine was too obvious —everybody would know that we shouldn't have dared to kill her."

"Well," said Griggs, "that's a line, of course. I wouldn't say it was a very strong one. There's such a

thing as a sudden temptation, following on long resentment and recent provocation. But let's stick to
facts. Now I ought to say that you don't have to comment on what I'm going to present to your notice;
the officer behind you there is taking notes; you don't
have to say a word."

"I'm sure I'll be quite willing to comment."

"Well: we have a statement here by a disinterested
witness, concerning a conversation you had with your
brother shortly after you met your stepmother for the
first time. Your brother is alleged to have said: 'This
is our big chance, Cora; but which of us will bump
her off?'"

Cora moved in her chair, and then sat rigid; so still
that she might have been holding her breath.

"Then," said Griggs, "your brother is alleged to
have said: 'She's worse than I expected. How about
using an ax?' To which you are alleged to have replied: 'Sh. Do you want to ruin us?'" Griggs looked
up from his notes. "Any comment on that, Miss Malcolm?"

She had relaxed. After a pause she said in a natural
tone: "No fair-minded person could take any of that
seriously. People wouldn't say that kind of thing if
they meant to commit murder. My brother says what
comes into his head; we have our jokes together, and
family jokes aren't always in good taste."

"You weren't taking him seriously when you asked
him if he wanted to ruin you both?"

"Of course I didn't want Mrs. Malcolm to hear him
say such things—or hear that he had said them. Mr.
Redfield wouldn't have repeated my brother's nonsense—I suppose it was one of the servants. As if he'd

risk being overheard if he meant to commit a murder!"

"The murder was committed when four other people were practically on the spot, and none of them in sight of anybody else."

"We couldn't know that."

"The murderer knew it somehow." Griggs consulted his papers again. "You don't have to tell me this, Miss Malcolm; did you or your brother have any special need at present for that extra two thousand a year?"

She said: "You mean for my father's money."

"Any extra money."

"I can only say what I said before; people want things as they get older that they could do without when they were young."

"You're pretty young yet."

"We got on very well in Paris on four thousand dollars a year."

"Living together?" She nodded. "I understand your brother's married; isn't living with his wife now. Paying alimony?"

"A separation allowance, I think they call it."

"We'll have him in now." Griggs rose.

Cora got up stiffly. "Lieutenant Griggs—I want to say again that you mustn't take everything my brother says too seriously. I don't know whether you know exactly what I mean, but he's a talker; he likes talk for its own sake, and sometimes his tongue runs away with him. He's extremely clever. I don't want you to be prejudiced against him if he says ridiculous things—he'd say them if he were dying."

"All right, Miss Malcolm."

When she had gone, and her brother had been sent for, Griggs returned to his chair looking incensed.

"Well," he said, "we've got our orders. We're not to pay any attention to what Malcolm says, because he'll say anything, and he's so bright we couldn't understand him anyway."

"I wonder whether she thinks that kind of thing is likely to do him much good," said Mosson. "I feel prejudice welling up in me already. Are you conscious of any bias against this paragon, Gamadge, or has he dazzled you?"

"We squared up in a refined way," admitted Gamadge, "and jabbed each other's vanity. But the pokes we exchanged didn't amount to much, and I don't think either of us felt resentment."

Malcolm came in a good deal as if he were entering a room in a museum; hands sunk in the pockets of his coat, expression mildly receptive, eyes wandering. He saw Gamadge.

"Ah," he said, "the collaborationist."

Gamadge smiled at him.

"Your place, sir," he continued, "is with us Partisans in the next room. We can't talk privately, we are under the benevolent but watchful eye of Officer Stromer, who won't join us in a drink." He eyed the bottle in front of Mosson. "Glad you are less doctrinaire in here."

"If you'll just come and sit where I can talk to you, Mr. Malcolm," said Griggs.

Malcolm went over to the row of chairs, and turned the farthest of them so that he faced everybody except Officer Ames. He sat down, placed his right ankle on his left knee, and clasped the ankle with a strong, smooth hand.

"I should tell you," he went on, "that we Partisans are committed to the Outsider theory. But our ranks are divided—we represent two schools of thought on the subject of the Outsider. Miss Ryder, Mrs. Drummond, and Mr. Drummond incline to the heresy of the Homicidal Maniac. My sister and I, more orthodox, prefer the thesis of the Avenger From The Past. Mrs. Malcolm's past. Both creeds are fantastic, we admit; but so was this crime. We don't know what Mr. Redfield thinks—he only joined us a few minutes ago, and is fussing about our comfort. He's been upstairs communing with functionaries."

Mosson said: "Perhaps the crime would seem less fantastic if we considered it as having been committed by somebody known to be present this afternoon."

"You must of course, not being Partisans but persons in authority, take that possibility into consideration," said Malcolm. "But we Partisans, not being allowed to talk privately, as I said, must in common decency to one another seem to accept the Outsider theory to the exclusion of all others.

"But even you, I suppose, don't consider Miss Ryder for a moment as a possible murderer. Nor Mr. Redfield—for more than two moments, say. Nor the Drummonds, who don't go about slaying strangers at cocktail parties. Nor my sister, if you're capable of judging character at all. No, I'm the person who interests you. But there's a flaw in the case against me. May I smoke a cigarette?"

Nobody voicing an objection, he took out his case and lighter, got a cigarette going, and went on:

"The gloves. Why should I have worn gloves? My hands were already stained, perhaps they still are. My prints were on the rifle. All I needed to do was—or would have been—to smudge those prints as they would have been smudged by a person wearing gloves. Much quicker than getting those gloves and putting them on."

Griggs, who had been listening to this flow of talk with a kind of disgusted fascination, now used a phrase which he had no doubt heard in courtrooms. "It may surprise you to learn, Mr. Malcolm, that we thought of that. But a murderer is nervous, and he wouldn't like to risk leaving a print somewhere that ought to have been smudged and missed being smudged. It's not such a quick job, thinking out the right places on a rifle to wipe off."

"You may be right; still, I think defense counsel might make something of my point."

"What would he make of the fact that you were heard to talk to your sister about bumping Mrs. Malcolm off, and using an ax?"

"Oh dear me," said Malcolm, after a short pause, "is that why Cora came away from the interrogation just now looking so dejected? Well, I think I can promise you one thing; if I'm ever tried for this murder, and those remarks of mine come out in cross-examination, the audience will laugh their heads off."

"You don't seem to worry much about the future."

"Oh, no."

Gamadge spoke in a tone of detachment: "Quote: *Mend your speech a little, Lest it may mar your fortunes.* Unquote."

Malcolm looked over at him smilingly. "Perhaps it *might* be as well for me to remember," he said cheerfully, "that Cordelia was hanged." He added, "The trouble is that I'm so used to tribunals. Europe in 1940, you know; Bureaux de Something or Other.

Pale Frenchmen, and then rosy Germans, and then busy Portuguese. One ends by adopting an airy pose."

Griggs said: "We might go back to nineteen forty now. You were living in Paris with your sister, I think, when war broke out?"

"Yes."

"Until the Germans came?"

"Yes. Until just before the Germans came."

"You had lived there some years?"

"About five. After we left our schools in England. Our schooling had been paid for out of the estate. No provision had been made for a university education for us."

"Any occupation in Paris, Mr. Malcolm?"

"None. We were rentiers—living on our incomes. The French don't consider that a serious blot on one's character, you know—to live on one's income."

"Did I understand that you and Miss Malcolm are writers?"

"At that time we put marks on paper; but we were of the vanishing school of perfectionists—we didn't intend to publish until we felt that we were ready. We were, as you must gather," he added, smiling, "literary snobs of the first class."

"You don't write now?"

"No." He put his hand to the back of his head with what seemed an automatic gesture, took it away again, and said: "We aren't perfectionists any more, and we probably never shall try to write again. As that Russian says, in that preposterous play I always liked, the rhythm of our lives has been broken. What I mean is, we're out of our literary element."

Griggs, after a stolid look at him, went on: "You decided to quit before the Germans came?"

"Yes. It took us some time to make up our minds to go—Paris was our home. But I finally decided that I didn't want Cora there after the invasion."

"You weren't married at that time, Mr. Malcolm?"

"No, that came later; it's part of the story of our exodus."

"Let's hear about it."

"Well, it wasn't easy. We hadn't much money, and no political pull; unfortunately such friends of ours as did have it were already friends with the Germans. I wonder what on earth is to become of those gifted beings now." He seemed to ruminate. "Nothing much physically, I suppose, and they're all so conceited that they won't mind anything else. Where was I? Oh: we ran like rabbits, and our gas gave out, and we were stuck on the route, and I'm sure you've heard variations on our story until you're sick of them. Pretty soon the war arrived—overhead, you know; we were machine-gunned from the air, and not very high up either. I woke in a ditch, with a head wound and a broken leg. Cora and a blond girl were dragging me out. Next thing I knew I was in a hospital in Bordeaux, with no sheets on the bed; and the blond girl—in nurse's uniform—was looking after me. She *was* a nurse; she'd been staying on in Paris with a rich American patient till the patient died."

"American herself?"

"Oh, yes. If it hadn't been for her I never should have come through alive; and I'm not so sure that Cora would have made it either. She had all her nurse's papers, and I was supposed to be her patient—the rich American, you know." He smiled. "And she got us priorities on transportation and food and so on; I never saw such drive. She got us through to Lisbon. Small, her name was; Frederica Small.

"Well, I was laid up in Lisbon a long time; couldn't have stood the trip to America." His pronunciation of the name, English with a touch of France, made him sound definitely a foreigner. "I wasn't walking yet," he went on, "and my head still bothered me a good deal. Freddy being a nurse, with a uniform, well! You've no idea what it did for us."

"Lucky for you she found you in that ditch."

"Lucky." He lighted another cigarette. "I married her in Lisbon; still in the hospital, you know, and not a good risk. But she was kind enough to accept the proposition, and that released Cora, who went on ahead by Clipper. And that's all."

Griggs said: "I understand you're now separated from your wife."

"Yes, but we're quite friendly. She drops in on us in New York when she's there, but she's fond of travel, and she has relatives in the Middle West."

"Too bad you had to break it up, after all you went through together, and all she did for you and your sister."

"Yes, wasn't it? But when she married me I was simply a recumbent object of charity, and when I got on my feet she didn't like me so well. I don't blame her. I'm much more agreeable when I'm ill."

"Did you break up after you reached this country, Mr. Malcolm?"

"Oh, yes. A year afterwards. We got here in the autumn of nineteen forty, and we separated the following year."

"Where is she now?"

"I don't know."

of course," he said, "Drum
colm girl would have been an un-
ation. She to do the shooting, he to

noise like a crow if anybody came along?"
miled. "Any two of them were an unbeatable
tion, Griggs; Mrs. Drummond and Malcolm,
field and anybody. But I'm for the Malcolms."
s worse than the old gang wars," said Griggs,
rly, "because there's nobody here to tip us off,
ept the servants, and Malcolm's right about the
irtz woman's evidence—all the prosecution would
et out of that would be a laugh."

look into the dining room. They we̶r̶e̶ helping themselves to food and drink fro̶m̶
and the sideboard. Officer Stromer loyal̶l̶y̶ ̶join-
ed the party, refusing coffee from Alice's ̶w̶i̶t̶h̶
detached and official air.

Gamadge lightly climbed to the second floor.

behind him. Then he said: "Ames, go get yourself
something to eat at that buffet. Ask then to send two
trays in here, and then come back youself." He came
from behind the table as Ames went out, sank dow
on the sofa beside Gamadge, and uttered: "Y
could go crazy."

"So you could," said Mosson, with sympath
you could."

"Mrs. Drummond's right; as thin And
have to arrest them both."

"My personal opinion is," said osson,
they're as guilty as the Macbeids. Cold fishes.
used that wife of his to get em out rance
then they ditched her—when the rhythm thei
got broken!" He looked at Gamadge. "Are ther
sat, and never opened your mouth except to
Malcolm a friendly warning."

"Didn't want him wasting your time with his
berish," explained Gamadge.

"He might have gone on and talked himself in
trouble," show-off like that."

Griggs was frowning. "O
mond and the Mal
beatable combir
scout for her'.

"Make a
Mosson

Gamadge rose. "Try it as a solo," he said. "You don't often g_ two murderers in a crowd like this— _t in the ru_of the cards. I'm still interested in Miss _h."

_le it thard way, don't you?" Griggs scowled

_wo_red whether you'd be willing for me _ddress _6k around the room—Mrs. Malcolm's _fects o_ _tination among Mrs. Malcolm's _ight be some trace of Gouch's past "Not for uch. Or l you_ _ked through everything?" _ck to G_ head," said Griggs, "and good _rough." The do_'s unlocked; the M.E. is "I'll just_ _have a look before I patronize the buffet _nd take _Aby home."

"The Dr_mmonds are going to have to stay tonight," said Griggs. "I might as well hang on to what I've got till after the inquest, anyhow."

"Much better," agreed Gamadge.

He went out through the living room, which he _ _d the hall, and had a discreet _ _were all there, help- _ _m the long table _ _r superintend- found _ _ray with a

"No, I really don't." He added: "Subsequent events drove that kind of thing from my mind."

"I'm not trying to catch you out, Mr. Malcolm; Mrs. Drummond was definite about the conversation."

"I should corroborate if I could. Does it matter?"

"Perhaps not. Did you see her go into the greenhouse?"

"No, I didn't. I started down the road and never looked back."

"See Mr. Redfield?"

"I dimly remember a glimpse of him stooping among his cabbages."

"But you didn't get a glimpse of Mr. Drummond when you went through the flower garden?"

"No, but that's just cutting across a corner from one gate to another."

"Mr. Malcolm, why did you go down to the swimming pool?"

"I like it there."

"*You* didn't go there expecting to find flowers to cut for Mr. Redfield?"

"Never thought of such a thing until I saw those wild asters."

"It was a party; a party for your stepmother. Yet you go off to the bottom end of the property and stay there by yourself for twenty minutes."

"Our host absented himself; I probably took his procedure to mean that the party as a party was over, and that we might all do as we pleased."

Griggs rose. "That's all for now."

Malcolm, with what seemed like relief, got up and walked to the door. He opened it and went out with no backward glance; Griggs watched the door close

"You don't keep in touch with this lady, Mr. colm?" Griggs' tone was one of dry surprise.

"She keeps in touch with me. She knows where am, and I never know where she is."

"Neither of you wants a divorce?"

"Well, really," said Malcolm, "I don't know why that question should enter into this investigation. But I'll answer it by saying that the matter is entirely in her hands."

"Young people—I should think you'd want a fresh start."

Malcolm, his eyes on the tip of his cigarette, might not even have heard this remark. Griggs, after a long and lowering stare at him, turned back to his notes. When he looked up again he spoke casually:

"Exactly what did you do, Mr. Malcolm, after you hung up the dead crows outside that gate?"

Malcolm answered readily: "I went down the road to the lower gate, went through the garden, went through the orchard, and went down to the swimming pool."

"Didn't you talk to anybody first?"

"A word or two with Mrs. Drummond. She stopped on her way to the greenhouse."

"What did you talk about?"

Malcolm, looking surprised, said he didn't remember. "Just a passing word."

"You don't remember that she excused herself from going down to the swimming pool with you, as you'd arranged to do?"

Malcolm studied him. Then he said: "No, it's slipped my mind."

"Don't remember her excuse? That she'd spoil her shoes?"

10

The Best Room

It was dim upstairs, but Gamadge remembered the arrangement of the rooms very well. Before the wings had been put on, a broad hall had run from the front to the back of the square house, with two bedchambers and a bath on one side of it, two smaller rooms, a series of cupboards and the stair landing on the other. The attics had accommodated such help as lived in; but Redfield now used them for storage, thinking them too hot in summer for human occupation. Now a cross corridor bisected the main hall and ran north and south, giving access to the rooms in the new wings.

But though these rooms were modern, some of them luxurious, none was as impressive as the old best chamber over the dining room. It had always been the best bedroom in the Redfield house, and it retained its fine solid furniture and its great fourpost curtained bed. Redfield, Gamadge thought, would certainly have put his Aunt Josephine in it. She would have respected it of old.

He was surprised to find its door open; for, dim as the light was, he could see that it was indeed a chamber of death. The shaded lamp on a dresser hardly brought out the subdued colors in the handsome flowered hangings and upholstery, and the bed curtains hung to the carpet, but he made out the sheeted figure of the dead woman.

He went across and looked down on it. The sheet was turned back from the face, which was enclosed in bandages like cerements. A strip crossed the forehead, concealing the bullet hole, and another bound up the chin. Like ancient cerements; there should have been tapers here, and watchers. But the sun worshiper had none.

Or had she none? Gamadge liked to describe himself as a mere bundle of nerves, but if the description had been accurate he might now have shrieked and fainted. Instead, he stood motionless as a figure detached itself from the shadows at the bed's head and looked at him across the body.

After some moments he put out his hand and turned the switch of a lamp on the bedside table beside him. This was no wraith or fetch, but a decidedly human being; a youngish woman, rather tall and buxom, with a white skin and a high color, and yellow hair surmounted by a jaunty hat. She was eying him coolly. At last she spoke in a sharp voice slightly subdued: "Are you Mr. Redfield?"

"No. I'm a guest."

She gave him no time to ask *his* question, but went on to explain her presence: "I saw people in the dining room when I passed the windows. I didn't care to mix with a party—I was looking for somebody I wanted to talk to privately. So I just came in and upstairs."

"You just . . . Excuse me. You're not here professionally, then?"

"Professionally?" She looked surprised, then

"No, I really don't." He added: "Subsequent events drove that kind of thing from my mind."

"I'm not trying to catch you out, Mr. Malcolm; Mrs. Drummond was definite about the conversation."

"I should corroborate if I could. Does it matter?"

"Perhaps not. Did you see her go into the greenhouse?"

"No, I didn't. I started down the road and never looked back."

"See Mr. Redfield?"

"I dimly remember a glimpse of him stooping among his cabbages."

"But you didn't get a glimpse of Mr. Drummond when you went through the flower garden?"

"No, but that's just cutting across a corner from one gate to another."

"Mr. Malcolm, why did you go down to the swimming pool?"

"I like it there."

"*You* didn't go there expecting to find flowers to cut for Mr. Redfield?"

"Never thought of such a thing until I saw those wild asters."

"It was a party; a party for your stepmother. Yet you go off to the bottom end of the property and stay there by yourself for twenty minutes."

"Our host absented himself; I probably took his procedure to mean that the party as a party was over, and that we might all do as we pleased."

Griggs rose. "That's all for now."

Malcolm, with what seemed like relief, got up and walked to the door. He opened it and went out with no backward glance; Griggs watched the door close

"You don't keep in touch with this lady, Mr. Malcolm?" Griggs' tone was one of dry surprise.

"She keeps in touch with me. She knows where I am, and I never know where she is."

"Neither of you wants a divorce?"

"Well, really," said Malcolm, "I don't know why that question should enter into this investigation. But I'll answer it by saying that the matter is entirely in her hands."

"Young people—I should think you'd want a fresh start."

Malcolm, his eyes on the tip of his cigarette, might not even have heard this remark. Griggs, after a long and lowering stare at him, turned back to his notes. When he looked up again he spoke casually:

"Exactly what did you do, Mr. Malcolm, after you hung up the dead crows outside that gate?"

Malcolm answered readily: "I went down the road to the lower gate, went through the garden, went through the orchard, and went down to the swimming pool."

"Didn't you talk to anybody first?"

"A word or two with Mrs. Drummond. She stopped on her way to the greenhouse."

"What did you talk about?"

Malcolm, looking surprised, said he didn't remember. "Just a passing word."

"You don't remember that she excused herself from going down to the swimming pool with you, as you'd arranged to do?"

Malcolm studied him. Then he said: "No, it's slipped my mind."

"Don't remember her excuse? That she'd spoil her shoes?"

amused. "Oh—you mean am I from the morticians? No."

Gamadge said: "I really must get this straight. Stromer was in the dining room, we didn't expect callers. But why didn't you ring?"

"The front door wasn't locked, and there wasn't anybody in the hall. I thought I'd slip upstairs and find somebody's room. Somebody I know."

"And you walked in on a corpse. It doesn't seem to have upset you!"

"I'm a trained nurse. I don't scream and run at sight of a body. Who's dead?"

Gamadge, studying her, asked: "Can you be Mrs. David Malcolm?"

"Certainly I am."

"You weren't expected, I think."

"No." She smiled. "But Dave and Cora might have expected me."

"You—er—came along to find out whether they actually did get two thousand more a year apiece from their stepmother?"

"Certainly I did. Dave said they'd been promised it, but it might have been six months before he let me know, and I can use some extra money myself."

"Of course you'd have a claim on some of it."

"I certainly would."

"He didn't know you were in this neighborhood today, I think you said?"

"He knew I'd come up if I found out when they were coming. I found out. Listen: would you mind telling me who this was, and why they're having a party about it? Is it a wake?"

"This is Mrs. Archibald Malcolm."

Her eyes opened until he saw a ring of whites

around the blue, and she looked at him dumbly. Then, almost in a whisper, she asked: "The *stepmother?*"

"Yes."

She gazed down at the peaked face framed in its white dressings, then at him again. "You mean they get all the money now?"

"Presumably."

"What—what killed the woman? Heart? Stroke?"

"I'll show you."

While she stood watching him and chewing at her lower lip, he leaned forward and gently turned back the gauze from the yellowish forehead.

When Mrs. David Malcolm saw the bullet hole her mouth fell open. As he replaced the gauze she straightened to stare at him again. He pulled the sheet over the dead face.

"Do you mean"—she got it out slowly—"it's a murder?"

"No doubt about that."

She drew in her breath, and then seemed to draw on her almost limitless reserves of self-possession: "Well, who did it?"

"There's no evidence."

"There isn't?"

"No."

"What the dickens happened, then?"

"Your husband had been shooting crows. He left a loaded rifle where any of six people could have got hold of it. Somebody put gloves on to fire it."

"When?"

"At about five twenty-six this afternoon."

"Whereabouts?"

"Have you ever been here before, Mrs. Malcolm?"

"No. I never put foot in the place until a few minutes ago."

"Then you wouldn't quite understand why the murderer wasn't seen. Would you tell me—I don't ask out of idle curiosity, I'm supposed to be more or less investigating the problem—when you arrived in Rivertown, if you came up by train?"

She thought his question over, her eyes on his greenish ones. Suddenly she looked amused. "I get it. They're trying to make out an outsider got in."

"Well—you did, although the place is now overrun by police."

"Well. Now isn't it just too bad!"

"Isn't what too bad?"

"Wait till you hear. You'll laugh, it's one on me."

"Go ahead and tell me the joke."

"I took the twelve twenty-seven from New York, as soon as a certain party in the Malcolms' apartment house telephoned me that they'd started off for the country. I missed their train, and got the next. That twelve twenty-seven was awful, but the only train I could get. It's Sunday, and it was jammed! I got to Rivertown at three-two, and found there was no bus out this way for an hour. I asked around in the station until they told me where I might hire a bike."

"A bike!"

"Yes, isn't that the limit? Some trail I left, didn't I?"

"I mean how on earth did you find a bike to hire on a Sunday?"

"I can get anything I want, any day of the week."

"So I gathered from your husband's description of how you got him and his sister out of France."

She gave him a cynical look from half-closed eyes, but made no comment on that. She went on:

"I got the bike at the drugstore where I got a container of coffee and some crullers; the clerk's brother rented it to me. They know when I rode off, and they got some fun out of it, too. These skirts we wear now, you could ride a fence rail in them; a few inches more leg, who cares?

"The point was, I like a picnic, and I didn't want to break in on the doings here too early. Those two—Dave and Cora—I wanted to give them plenty of time to get it all settled about the extra money, and then I was going to drop in. In case the kids might have ruined the deal after all; you never know how they'll go on, fooling the way they do when they get together. I was going to see Mrs. Malcolm myself, if I had to. I know a lot about old ladies.

"But just tell me how I could have fixed it up worse for myself. Not that I care. They can't do a thing to me."

"You think the outsider theory too farfetched?"

"They can fool with it if they like, they won't get anywhere with that kind of business. But imagine how I fixed myself. The clerk fitted me out with a shopping bag to hang on the handle bars, and I telephoned this inn at Old Bridge for a room for tonight, and off I rode. Ten miles to go, and I took four hours to get here—it's well after eight!"

"How did you while away the time, Mrs. Malcolm?"

"In a field, up a nice country lane. I found a place in the sun halfway up a rock, and I had my snack and my coffee and some cigarettes. I had a nap. I never started off again till it got chilly after the sun went down."

She stopped, and looked down again at the dead woman. When she spoke again it was briskly: "Well, they've got the money, anyway."

Gamadge, slightly horrified, said that perhaps they had.

"I bet it was an accident."

"They've more or less abandoned that theory."

"Accident or no accident, those kids would never do a thing like this. Dave Malcolm is too smart to do it or let Cora do it. And he could talk a jury's ears off, anyhow."

"You won't worry, so long as they get the money?"

She smiled. "That's right. I won't worry."

"May I ask what you did with your bicycle?"

"Parked it against a tree after I pushed it up the lane. Boy. Am I hungry after that push. The kids always said that Mr. Redfield's a nice man; I'd better go down and meet him and ask for something to eat. You know, I think it's lucky I came."

"Because your husband's financial position is now so different?"

"Well, it's more fun to look forward to a lot of money than to a few more hundreds, isn't it?"

"I must say I admire your courage. It was already a legend; now I find it a living fact."

She smiled. "It takes more than a thing like this to scare me. And it takes a lot to scare those twins." She added: "And they don't do many foolish things."

"Canny, are they?"

"Scotch, all right!"

"Well, I strongly advise you to go down now and

introduce yourself to the police, and tell them your story."

"Where's Dave?"

"He was in the dining room a few minutes ago."

"I didn't see him when I looked in."

"He was up beside one of the windows."

"I'll go down and find the cops."

"You'll find the important one on the right when you reach the hall."

"Thanks." She walked around the bed and out into the hall. Gamadge, following, saw her down the stairs and practically into the arms of Officer Stromer. He heard his astonished bark and her cool reply, then returned to the best room and closed the door.

He turned on all the lights. Then he crossed the room to a small desk under the north window. It was of course empty of Mrs. Malcolm's papers—Griggs had them. It was spotlessly neat—Alice or Tilly would look to that. If it had ever contained a letter or memorandum providing a clue to the present whereabouts of Miss Gouch, Griggs would have found it by this time.

Gamadge went to the dresser and found Mrs. Malcolm's expensive alligator handbag in the top drawer. It contained her ration books, her keys, stamps, an old shopping list, a couple of dollars in change and several hundreds of dollars in bills. Redfield was probably right in thinking that her bank balance had not been depleted during the summer—she had come to Idlers well provided with cash; and no doubt she had settled most of her outstanding accounts in Pasadena before she left for her long visit East.

A small address book in the handbag did not supply the address, permanent or other, of Miss Gouch.

Had Mrs. Malcolm acquired her from a registry office or from an acquaintance or a friend? And would registry office or friend have her permanent address, or only that of her previous position? Could such persons as Miss Gouch be located at all during the summer months, between jobs?

The top drawer held gloves, monogrammed linen handkerchiefs, oddments, and two old jewel cases and a leather jewel box. In one of the jewel cases Redfield or somebody had replaced the diamond cluster which had been on the dead woman's breast; in the other were two rings which had sparkled on her fingers that afternoon. As custom orders, they had left her the wedding ring. Lesser ornaments were jumbled in the leather box—perhaps the heart-shaped pin had been among them, the Token which was now lost.

Other drawers in the dresser contained expensive, plain, handmade undergarments of prewar quality—Mrs. Malcolm would have had such a stock of them as should last the duration. They were of comfortable, elderly cut, and all monogrammed.

The dresser top had glass to cover its fine old polished surface. There was a framed photograph of a dour-looking man on it, a bearded man with pale eyes. No doubt Mr. Archibald Malcolm—his children had not inherited their coloring from him. Had they inherited the ruthless determination that showed in what could be seen of his tight mouth? Not a man of sentiment.

The handsome and costly, but plain, toilet articles on the dresser looked as if they might have belonged in a fitted traveling case. They, like Mrs. Malcolm's other personal belongings, were monogrammed—J.R.M. Gamadge found the traveling case—a fine but small pigskin one—in the larger of the two large cupboards. It contained no papers relating to Miss Gouch, and had no inner compartment for letters or jewelry. There were two other pieces of small luggage, and a small wardrobe trunk; this stood open in an angle of the cupboard, and was empty. No clue to the present whereabouts of Gouch here.

The other cupboard was fitted with hooks, and with shelves above and below. It held dresses and coats, robes, hats, slippers and shoes; a plain, conservative wardrobe except for three bright tea gowns or house robes and their matching sandals; Mrs. Malcolm had chosen them all of the same length and cut, and seemed to have liked cheerful colors in her negligees. One was pink, one blue, and here was the yellow one. It had no bloodstains on it, and had been hung up with the rest. A flannel bath gown near it had lost its cord—Gamadge found the cord attached to the yellow robe by a safety pin.

The yellow wreath had probably sunk long since to the bottom of the rock pool, but on the shelf, among other hats, was the straw shade-hat it had been taken from.

There was nothing in any pocket of coat or robe or dressing gown.

Gamadge closed the cupboard door, and without looking again at the sheeted figure on the bed went out of the best room. He closed its door behind him, and turned right. When he reached the entrance to the north wing he turned right again, and walked the length of the wing to the back stairs. Descending them, he followed a passageway that led past kitchen and pantries to a lobby. One of its doors gave on the terrace, the other on the dining room; he found the latter empty, but the buffet supper had not been cleared away, and the coffee urn was still steaming.

He helped himself to cold beef and salad, bread and butter, fruit and cake, and filled a cup with coffee. Then, drawing up a chair, he sat down comfortably to his meal.

When he had finished, he crossed the hall—Stromer, he was amused to note, now guarded the front door—and went into the living room. Peace reigned there. So far as any newcomer could have guessed, no murder had been committed that afternoon, and no outsider had arrived at Idlers. The Partisans were following their chosen line.

Miss Ryder had in her characteristic fashion found herself something to do; she had laid out a patience on a small table to the right of the fireplace, and was busy at it; firmly disregarding Redfield's advice and censure, and ignoring the officious forefinger with which he pointed out combinations that she had missed. He was hanging over the back of her chair; anxious and worried, still badly shaken, but still able to play up as a host.

Blanche Drummond sat on an ottoman at the left of the hearth; she was doing nothing; and her eyes wandered. Walter Drummond stood behind her, his arm on the mantelshelf. He was smoking, and he watched Abigail's game.

David Malcolm sat in the west window seat, reading. His sister, on the east window seat, sat looking out on the darkness of the terrace.

Gamadge joined her; if the Partisans could behave as though nothing had happened, then so could he.

"You were born in Oregon, I think, Miss Malcolm?"

"Yes. My father had a place near Portland."

"Do you remember it?"

"Pretty well. It was a wonderful place for children. I often think of it."

The disinherited, how often they think of it! Gamadge said reflectively: "I'm cursed with the sense of the past, too."

"Are you?" She turned her head to look at him. "I didn't mean that I was, exactly. In fact, I'm not. I only think of the place in Oregon as a scene. It's because we have no roots." She added: "I mean that's why my brother and I have no sentiment about the past. We were never at home anywhere—we were foreigners. We didn't belong anywhere, and no place belonged to us. But David thinks that's better for people; he thinks you get a broader point of view."

"He may be right. I haven't that point of view, so I can't tell. *I'm* a mere jelly of sentiment, you know."

"Are you? I shouldn't have thought it."

"Oh, yes. I see some piece of junk, and I become sad; to think that it was somebody's treasure once, and is now a treasure no longer to anyone."

"That is being sentimental!"

"Oh, I assure you . . ."

But she was looking beyond him, and her face had changed. Gamadge turned, to see Mrs. David Malcolm standing in the doorway, Lieutenant Griggs looming in her wake. She was smiling as her eyes passed from one occupant of the room to another; she looked very big in her short suit, which revealed a notable length of sturdy leg in mesh stockings. She looked very blond, with her little stylish hat perched on top of her tightly curled hair.

Redfield's face, as he took her in, was a blank of astonishment. He simply couldn't imagine who she was. Drummond looked surprised, too, Blanche Drummond merely shocked. Clothes like those Mrs. Malcolm wore really shocked her.

Malcolm rose, and he returned her smile. "Well, Freddy," he said, "I see you managed it. Do you feel rewarded?"

Her good-humored, cynical gaze fixed him keenly. "Just as well I came," she aid. "You kids need me to look out for you. I bet if I'd been here this afternoon none of it would have happened."

11

The Outsider

Johnny Redfield, after no more than a few seconds of astonishment, hurried forward. "Good heavens, you must be Mrs. David."

"That's right." She cast a merry glance in her husband's direction, and took Redfield's proffered hand.

"But I had no idea you were in the neighborhood." He looked as if this new complication were almost more than he could grasp.

"Neither had Dave and Cora." She smiled.

"How ghastly; to meet you for the first time in these circumstances," said Johnny, trying his best to keep things on the social plane.

"Yes, it's bad, isn't it? I was flabbergasted when I heard," said Mrs. David cheerfully.

"But when did you come?"

"About an hour ago. I biked from Rivertown."

"Biked! I could have sent somebody. I should have managed it."

"I bet you would. The kids always said you were mighty nice. Their best friend."

"I've tried to be a friend to them. Do sit down, Mrs. David. You must be exhausted." He glanced about him as if distraught, and at last urged her towards a sofa against the wall opposite the fire. But when they reached it he stopped.

"Am I quite out of my mind? Let me introduce you. Miss Ryder, Mrs. Drummond, Drummond, and our friend Henry Gamadge."

She nodded coolly to each, but when her eyes met Gamadge's she favored him with a broad grin. He returned it.

"And you must have something to eat. Or have you had your supper somewhere?" asked Redfield. "I don't—I simply cannot believe that you biked from Rivertown!"

"Oh, I did. But I've had supper. When I came, the cops got me."

"Cops? Oh. You mean you've been talking to Griggs." Redfield seemed for the first time aware of Griggs in the doorway. The lieutenant withdrew into the hall and out of sight.

"Yes," said Mrs. David Malcolm. "And to somebody in plain clothes."

"Plain clothes?"

"But he's left. A man named Mosson."

"Oh. Yes. Our State's Attorney."

"Funny guy. We had a laugh or two when I told them about my trip here. But that Mosson would get a laugh out of the dead march. Anyway, they were having a tray. They sent the trooper out to get me something. I haven't tasted such a piece of beef since the fall of forty-one."

"Well, I'm very glad indeed that you were taken care of." He settled her on the sofa and sat beside her—a perfect host in difficulties. "David, my boy, it's quite time for drinks. The maids have had a long

day, we won't disturb them. You know your way
about the pantry. Will you bring us the usual tray?"

"Delighted." As he crossed the room, his wife
watched him. When he had gone, she turned to Redfield; now serious and sympathetic, she showed for
the first time what must have been part of her professional quality: "Mr. Redfield, this is a terrible thing.
If there weren't any ladies present I'd say a hell of a
thing."

"Yes, it's very bad for us all."

"The cops don't seem to know what they're doing."

"They're puzzled; we all are. Now of course you'll
be staying tonight. Let me see—we must rearrange—"

"Oh, no, thanks," said Mrs. David. "I have a room
engaged in the inn at Old Bridge. I'll just get on my
bike and go there. I'll be coasting half the way, from
what I remember of the trip up."

"But I absolutely must insist—"

"No, thanks. I have no luggage or anything, and I
wouldn't put you out for anything. You must be
pretty well upset now."

"Well, the Drummonds are staying; but—did you
get your suitcases, Blanche?"

Blanche Drummond, who had been gazing at Mrs.
David Malcolm as if in a fearful fascination, said yes,
the suitcases had come.

"The Drummonds have the suite next to mine, in
the south wing," chattered Redfield, "with a bath between. I could put you in the corner room, and you
could share the bath with Mrs. Drummond. And Walter Drummond could go into the yellow room at the
head of the stairs, and share *my* bath."

"No, thanks," repeated Mrs. David. "I haven't even
a toothbrush."

"I might lend you something, Freddy," said Cora Malcolm in a dry voice.

"I'd split the seams, dearie," said Mrs. Malcolm. "No, I'll just wander off. The cops want me to come back tomorrow, so I'll be here. It's mighty kind of you, Mr. Redfield, but when you come right down to it, I wasn't invited and there isn't any reason from your point of view that I should have been. I guess everybody including myself will be perfectly satisfied to have me down at the inn."

Malcolm came in carrying a big silver tray, which he had loaded with a siphon, a bottle of whisky, glasses, and ice. He set it down on the table which Abigail had cleared of her cards. Redfield got up and went to help him pour drinks.

"Are the police making you stay here?" asked Mrs. David, addressing Gamadge with a certain interest.

"No, my cousin Abigail and I are going home. She lives just down the hill." Gamadge came to light her cigarette.

"What lets you out?" she inquired in a confidential tone.

"We didn't know the deceased lady well enough to murder her," replied Gamadge, also lowering his voice.

"That's why they're letting me off."

Redfield had approached with her highball, and caught her last remark. "But why on earth *should* they detain you, Mrs. David?" he asked.

She took the glass from him and drank some of its contents with every sign of gratification. Then she wiped her lips with her handkerchief and answered Johnny in her earlier manner—the raffish one: "Well, I got to Rivertown a little early, at three-two. I had a picnic in the woods, and I kept off the highways, and I might have been right on hand when the tragedy occurred. They don't think I was, of course, but they want me to stick around until they find the other outsider—the one that really shot Mrs. Archibald Malcolm."

Everybody in the room was looking at her, and a long silence followed her speech. Then Blanche Drummond said: "What an extraordinary coincidence: Your happening to come up to Rivertown when you did, and then going off on a bicycle for the whole afternoon."

Mrs. David Malcolm took another gulp of highball, took another cigarette from a box offered by Gamadge, and looked about her. David Malcolm came forward with a lighted match. She accepted the light from him without acknowledgment, looked at Blanche Drummond through smoke, and then replied:

"No coincidence, Mrs. Er . . . I came up because I heard that my husband and his sister had come, and I knew they were coming to meet their stepmother. I wanted to find out right away whether she was really going to give them two thousand apiece a year. I was interested. It would mean that I could live decently without wearing my feet off in some hospital. These war times, you have no idea; and I'm tired of private work."

"But nursing is such a wonderful job," said Blanche, in a gentle, admiring tone. "I don't see how you can want to give it up."

Mrs. David Malcolm looked at her for some moments, then drained her glass and put it down. "I'll try to get along without it," she said, "when Dave gets his money."

"If, Freddy, if!" Malcolm came and took her glass away to be refilled. "The word at present seems to be 'if.' My reversionary rights in my father's estate never looked more precarious."

"You're the damndest fool," observed his wife equably. "Never mind, I've got you and Cora out of worse jams than this, you might remember. I'll stick around and get you out of this one."

Cora said: "Freddy, did you really think we'd try to cheat you?"

Redfield, unable to bear the turn the conversation had taken, sputtered: "Mrs. David! These young people—always speak of you with the deepest gratitude. We all know what you did for them—"

She interrupted in her casual way: "Nineteen forty is a long time ago, Mr. Redfield."

Abigail got up. "I'll be going on home, Johnny. Telephone me tomorrow when I'm wanted."

He went up to her and took her hands: "Abby, I can't tell you how much I regret all this for you!"

"It's not as bad for me as for the rest."

"I'll just get you a torch."

He bustled after her into the hall. Gamadge drained his highball, said good night, and followed them, to find Griggs assisting at the conversation in the living room from the wings—i.e., a position outside the door—while Redfield rooted in the stair cupboard and Abby waited on the front doorstep.

Griggs took hold of Gamadge's arm: "Would you come back?"

"I you want me. Why?"

"This woman—this Mrs. David Malcolm. I'd like to

talk her over. I can't make her out. She hasn't a ghost of an alibi, and you might say she has a motive, and her excuse for being here is thin. But she's so cocky I don't make her out. I'm having them watch her to Old Bridge, and watch the inn."

"I supposed you would."

"Can you come back after you've seen Miss Ryder home?"

"If you like, of course."

Johnny produced the torch, and Gamadge and Abigail went off into the freshness of the night. Abigail, who never risked being overheard by persons she wished to discuss, waited until they had left the house behind, and then spoke in a tone of quiet horror:

"That frightful woman. That nurse."

"Not a type you're accustomed to, Abby."

"Can it be a type? I shouldn't think there could be others! Where can she have come from? She's a barbarian; where can she have had her training?"

"You can remain quite a barbarian if you really try, training or no training," said Gamadge.

"That unfortunate boy couldn't have been more than twenty-one or -two when she roped him in."

"I suppose he was glad enough to hang on to that rope she threw him when he was in that ditch on the French road."

"Any decent human being would do what she did for them if possible. And she reminds them of it!"

"Ought they to need reminding?"

"How old can she be?"

Gamadge's torch was picking out pine cones and fallen leaves on the trail. He said: "About Blanche Drummond's age, probably. Thirty-five, I should say."

Abby was silent for a minute. At last she said: "I hope you don't mean to compare them?"

"Well—I don't think, Abby, that Mrs. David Malcolm is any tougher than Blanche is about money."

"Henry, how can you talk like that? How can you? Think of that marriage! He was probably half out of his wits in that hospital, and his sister couldn't bear the match and came home first. Blanche—Blanche—she's just lost her head. She'll get over it. It's just a fancy. It's not for *money*. How could it be, when he's so obviously tired of the whole thing?"

"You saw the whole thing?"

"Certainly not; just a glimpse or two last summer and today."

"Until now it's been the men who have run after Blanche. Do you think she'll easily believe that he can be tired—for keeps?"

"I certainly don't believe that Blanche Drummond would commit a crime for money!"

"You only think Mrs. David Malcolm would because she's so ill-bred."

"Henry, you do annoy me. Wouldn't you *prefer* it to be Mrs. David Malcolm?"

Gamadge said gloomily that if it came to that he never liked to see bounders brought low. "Unless they're criminals, of course; and even then it's so awful when they cringe."

"I never can make you out. It's much more tragic for the other kind."

"Exactly. And they can stand it better."

Miss Ryder stopped talking; it was in silence that they arrived at the cottage.

Gamadge saw her safely in, saw that her old cook was in, lighted lights, locked windows, told Abigail to

forget about him until morning, and at a quarter to
ten climbed the hill back to Idlers.

When he reached the gap in the Redfield hedge he
noticed a faint wandering light somewhere in the
grounds. He put his face against the wire where he
had put it that afternoon, and was startled when the
figure of Apollo shone out from the darkness, glowing
as with the phosphorescence of decay. The light vanished, to reappear lower down, and Gamadge remembered that there was a policeman in the grounds.

"I'm getting the creeps, as usual," he told himself,
"and why not?"

He found the kitchen end of the house in darkness,
and saw a light in the Debenhams' cottage. They had
finished work for tonight.

Stromer open the front door for him. "Mr. Redfield
and the lieutenant are in the studio," he said. "Everybody else went up to bed early—Mrs. Drummond quit
first and started the rest of them. That blonde of Malcolm's was too much for the party."

Gamadge, raising an eyebrow, went through the living room to find Griggs slowly pacing the length of
the studio, and Redfield sitting near the fire. He
looked up. "Well, Gamadge, thank God the day's almost over. Get yourself a drink, will you, if you want
one? I'm exhausted. That woman—she's too much for
me. How did the boy ever bring himself—but those
are the things one never understands. I don't know
what I supposed she was like—some untutored little
person, harmless but tiring, with a certain ephemeral
charm. But this . . . ! Griggs, why don't you
drop all the nonsense about the Malcolm children,
and concentrate on her? She's truly terrifying. She'd

do anything. She's probably murdered half a dozen rich patients for their cash and jewelry."

"I'm concentrating on her," said Griggs. "Gloves, for instance—a nurse would think of gloves right away. She packed a gun in France, told me so. Doesn't care what she tells me. She's so impudent that I'm afraid she *has* an alibi, and wants us to arrest her and make fools of ourselves. She just grins at me and asks how she could have known she'd get a shot at Mrs. Malcolm with a rifle. And if she's in collusion with those twins, all I can say is that they're all better actors than Shakespeare."

Nobody correcting this slip, he went on:

"Wasn't it Malcolm that suggested the crow shooting, Mr. Redfield?"

"He simply expressed a wish for a rifle, after I'd complained of the crows. I was as much to blame for the crow shooting as he was. Shouldn't you say so, Gamadge?"

Gamadge replied that as he remembered it, the whole thing was quite casual and unpremeditated.

"The woman asked me that question," said Redfield, "while I was taking her up to her room."

Gamadge, who had an arm on the mantel, gripped the ledge with his hand as he turned to look down at the speaker. "While you *what?*"

"Oh, that's true, you aren't abreast with the times at all." Redfield made a face of wry amusement. "She stayed."

"Mrs. David Malcolm is staying here tonight?"

"Didn't you hear me invite her?" Redfield gave a short laugh.

"But she refused; and I must say, Johnny, that although you were doing your best, your invitation was perfunctory." Gamadge's hand dropped from the mantelshelf, and he sat down opposite Redfield. "She reconsidered?"

"Well, you'll be as surprised as I was, Gamadge; Blanche persuaded her."

Gamadge stared.

"Fact, absolute fact, and I was never so surprised in my life. After you'd gone she came and sat down beside Mrs. David, told her how rotten the inn is—it's no great shakes, I'm afraid, they don't seem to have even their quota of meat, unless they eat it all themselves—and said she had a little silk wrapper in her bag that Mrs. David could certainly use for a night-gown."

"And Malcolm's wife accepted the offer of the little silk wrapper and the other half of Blanche's suit?"

"Yes; she said she liked the idea of a good bed after all. So Blanche went up to unpack the wrapper, and I took Mrs. David up and installed her. I didn't rout out poor Tilly. I apologized for it, or tried to, but Mrs. D. wouldn't listen; said she was capable of turning her own bed down. Blanche came in with the wrapper, Mrs. D. approved, and Blanche retired. I investigated the stores in the bathroom, and then bowed myself out."

Gamadge said after a pause: "If it's not too much of an imposition, Johnny, I'll ask you to put *me* up—a sofa will do."

"My dear boy, delighted. Sofa? You'll be comfortable on the day bed in my study upstairs, and we shan't bother each other—the bath's between us. But . . ." He frowned. "May I ask why? The woman may very well be a murderer, and I'm not too happy about having her here; but we have Stromer, and we have Griggs."

Griggs had paused in his march. He said with a smile: "Perhaps Mr. Gamadge is thinking that if anything happened to Malcolm his wife could come into half the Malcolm money."

"She would," agreed Gamadge, "if anything short of conviction of murder happened to him."

"Don't worry. Even if she's the homicidal maniac Redfield's friends have been hoping for," said Griggs dryly, "she wouldn't try anything until the house was quiet. It isn't quiet yet. They all went up early, just after half-past nine, and it isn't a quarter past ten."

Gamadge said: "Not much in the idea, I agree with you, but I'll go up now."

Griggs said irritably: "Mr. Gamadge, I think you're—"

But Gamadge was never to know what Griggs thought of him. A broken, rising scream made them all jerk up their heads to stare at the ceiling, and then they made a run for the studio door. Gamadge was nearest it, and was on Stromer's heels as he dashed up the stairs.

The screaming came from the south wing. Drummond appeared in his doorway as Gamadge passed it, clad in pajamas and looking half awake. He joined the runners. Cora Malcolm, standing in *her* doorway, gazed after them. David Malcolm ran down the north corridor.

"Blanche!" shouted Drummond. "Blanche! That's Blanche!"

Stromer had reached her door, and hammered on it. He panted: "She don't answer. And it's locked."

"Break it down," shouted Drummond, pushing forward.

"No, no," gasped Redfield. "Quicker through Mrs. David's room."

They streamed back to the main hall, and around an angle. Griggs was first at a door opposite Cora Malcolm's; he turned the knob and went in.

He stopped short for a moment, and Gamadge could see over his shoulder. Blanche Drummond stood in the bathroom doorway and across the room; her hands clasped her head, her mouth was open, her hair tumbled on her shoulders. She wore a tailored satin robe, long and trailing. Her staring eyes were fixed on the body of Mrs. David Malcolm, which lay face downwards between her and the bed. It was fully dressed, except for the hat, which lay with her handbag on a table near the windows, and its arms were outstretched and pointing towards the bath. The yellow hair, thick and curly, was matted and stained.

The bed extended from the wall beside the doorway; near it and on the floor lay a bronze, vase-shaped lamp, its cord still attached to the plug in the baseboard. Its shade had fallen off, and Griggs had stepped on it.

12

Easy

Blanche Drummond lifted her eyes from the body that lay almost at her feet, but her witless stare did not fix itself on Griggs or on the crowd pressing behind him; it wandered. She put her arms out in front of her as if she were groping, and her knees gave way. Drummond shouldered past Griggs and caught her as she fell.

He carried her through the bathroom, and kicked the door of her bedroom shut behind him. Griggs watched him go with a scowl, but did not protest. He knelt down on one knee beside the dead woman, while Stromer shoved Gamadge aside and stood with his arms across the doorway.

But Gamadge had seen the long and narrow bed jutting out on the right, the night table which had held the lamp, the fallen lamp itself. A murderer need have been only a step within the room to strike Mrs. Malcolm down as she turned away.

Gamadge had seen something else. A light candle-wick spread had covered bed and pillow loosely; it now lay in a crumpled mass, as if it had been snatched up and flung down again.

Bright light came from a wall bracket over the dresser, and fell on flowered wallpaper, white curtains, white-painted furniture. Not a guest room of the first class, according to Redfield's standards, but a pleasant one, and spotless until now. Not a big room, since the bath had been sliced off it when it had been incorporated into the guest suite of the new wing.

Centrally located, too, opposite Cora Malcolm on the main corridor. Drummond's room was not far along at the head of the stairs, Malcolm's down the north wing, a few yards away.

Griggs looked over his shoulder: "Stromer, get these people downstairs. No: telephone. Then get hold of the outside man, and come back and get the crowd into the studio. Nobody's to leave the hall until you're back. Redfield?"

"Yes." Johnny stood in the hall beside the Malcolms, his face vacant and pale.

"You'll have to go with the rest. I'm no doctor, but I've seen a lot of bodies and I've seen a lot of blood. This woman has been dead nearer three-quarters of an hour than one, and you were upstairs just after nine-thirty, and you didn't join me in the studio until a couple of minutes before ten." He rose. "And she hadn't had time to take her clothes off." He cast a stony look at the hat and handbag on the table, and at the silk wrapper, a rosy affair of thin figured material, which hung over a chair.

Redfield said confusedly: "Of course. My God. Anything."

Stromer had already pounded down to the hall, and was dialing.

"Gamadge," said Lieutenant Griggs.

"Yes."

"Go and rout that Wirtz woman out and send her along to see after Mrs. Drummond. Tell Drummond he's to go down to the studio. If he objects, let me know. Time's past for that kind of thing and making exceptions."

Gamadge turned. Redfield stood listless as if incapable of thought or motion; he did not look at the Malcolms. They seemed quite stunned themselves. Shoulder to shoulder, dressed in dark robes over pajamas—silk robes of the same Chinese brocade pattern, though his was brown, hers plum-colored—they were like two youths from another century, brothers of the Renaissance.

Malcolm said: "You didn't hear anything, Cora?"

She shook her head. "We were talking, you remember."

"Talking, talking," said Malcolm, with a faint smile.

"You wouldn't hear anything," muttered Johnny. "Thick walls, thick doors; oh Lord, oh Lord."

Gamadge went down the north corridor. He glanced into Malcolm's open doorway as he passed it. There were books on a table, and most of them were paper-covered and French. Not Redfield's. Redfield's tastes were limited. Malcolm was evidently one of those persons who doesn't travel, even for a night, without his books.

It was difficult to make Tilly hear his knock; very difficult—when she did open the door—to make her understand what had happened and what was wanted of her. Aghast, she stood in her magenta woolen dressing gown and her red felt slippers with pompoms, her hair in a pink net, and looked at him from glassy, watering, pale-blue eyes. But when she did understand, she accepted the situation in a way that Gamadge could only think of as cosmopolitan. Anything can happen in Middle Europe, everything has happened; why not here?

"Who killed the lady?" was her only question, and it was asked with more interest than anxiety. Whoever it was wouldn't kill *her*, if she kept out of the way.

"The police will find out. Did you see her, Tilly?"

"No, but Alice said she was de wife Mr. Malcolm peeked up in Europe." Tilly added: "Dey peek dem up sometimes, de young men."

The comment was adequate, and covered all that had been said in the kitchen about the late Mrs. David Malcolm.

Gamadge waited in the hall until Tilly was dressed, and then took her past Stromer to the first door in the south wing. He waited outside until she had gone in, heard her sympathetic voice murmur that something was too bad, and heard Drummond reply.

Gamadge called: "Sorry, Walter; we're wanted downstairs."

Drummond came out; he looked ghastly.

"Blanche is knocked right out," he said. "She ought to have a doctor, but she won't let me send for one. She ought to go home. Two dead women in the house, and now a lot more policemen. They can't ask her questions. She ought to be sent home."

Gamadge made no reply. They went downstairs, found an officer in the lower hall, the one Gamadge had met that afternoon in the grounds, and were formally passed by him into the living room. Griggs was standing in front of the fire, Redfield sat collapsed on the settee.

"Oh—Drummond," said Griggs, "will you go on into the studio?"

Drummond went into the studio and shut the door.

"I got them all down here," said Griggs in his new angry tone, "so that Stromer could go through their rooms and baths. But they all had plenty of time to get off any blood they got on themselves—whatever can be got off. There's none on that spread; I suppose it was grabbed up and used as a screen, but it wasn't needed. We're having people up to make a regular search, a woman for Mrs. Drummond and Cora Malcolm. No use. Well, Mr. Gamadge: Mrs. David Malcolm didn't kill her stepmother-in-law, and she wasn't intending to kill her husband. And nobody got in this time!"

"No," said Gamadge. He sat down opposite Redfield and got out his cigarettes.

"It's right in the family this time. The woman did come here earlier today than she said she did, and she was down in the grounds, and she saw enough to tell her who killed Mrs. Archibald Malcolm. After she went upstairs she got a word with the party, and I suppose she tried blackmail. Would you put that past her?"

"From what I saw of her, no."

"Tough enough for that, wasn't she? And that's why she was so pleased with herself. She didn't lose a minute, and neither did he. A minute? He didn't lose a second. She probably hadn't more than got the words out of her mouth before he brained her."

"He waited for her to turn away," said Gamadge.

"And if you'll excuse me, Griggs," said Johnny, "you're not thinking clearly. How could she blackmail David Malcolm? She couldn't give him away— he'd lose the money if she did."

"Then who did she blackmail, Mr. Redfield?"

asked Griggs, and Redfield was silent. "Drummond? If you don't mind, let's stick to the man who always had the big motive, and no strings to it. I suppose you'll admit that Malcolm would have liked to get rid of her?"

"But it would be madness—"

"It was madness for anybody to do it. Now let's have your story again. You went up to her room with her. What exactly happened then?"

"She took off her hat, and put it and her bag down somewhere. Then while I poked around seeing that she had magazines to read, and cigarettes, and so on, she stood in front of the dresser and did something to her hair. Then Blanche came in and gave her the dressing gown; and she made some joke or other, you know that disagreeable kind of humor she had, about their both being blondes, and Blanche using a darker shade of dye than Mrs. David cared for. Blanche was very cool and civil. She went off, and I looked into the bathroom and then left."

"You turned on that light when you first came in?"

"Yes. There's a switch just beside the door."

"How long were you in there, would you say?"

"Five minutes, not much more."

"Now I expect frankness, Mr. Redfield: did she say anything about wanting a word with her husband?"

"No, I swear she didn't, Griggs. She said she was tired. No wonder."

"It was early."

"She said she was going to read. Something or other—one of the fashion magazines, I think—caught her fancy."

"So far as you know, then, she was in there for the night?"

"Yes."

"And Mrs. Drummond hadn't acted as if she intended to go back and have a chat with her?"

"Good heavens, no."

"But she did go back."

"Blanche will explain that."

"I hope so. You went along to your rooms, then. You couldn't hear anything, if there had been anything to hear?" As Redfield looked inquiring, Griggs added: "The murderer would think you were in your suite for the night."

"Oh—yes. No, I wouldn't hear anything. The suite is self-contained, you know, only one door. You go in by way of the study, and there's the bath and then my bedroom. Planned so that I *shouldn't* hear anything— the servants, or the vacuum cleaner, or my guests if they played the radio downstairs."

"You were in there at least twenty minutes, Mr. Redfield, before you came down to the studio to talk to me and wait for Gamadge."

"It was early, Griggs, as you reminded me just now. I couldn't think of bed. I had plenty of things to occupy me. I tried to listen to my radio, and I tried to look up papers and memoranda about the family plot, you know; I supposed I should bury my poor aunt in the plot in Old Bridge cemetery. I didn't know what arrangements she had made elsewhere, but I thought she probably had made none. I tried to write out a list of things I ought to do tomorrow. No good. I gave up and came downstairs."

"*You* didn't want to talk to the Malcolms?"

"No; I didn't. I thought they'd prefer to be left to themselves."

Griggs tapped the mantelshelf with heavy fingers.

"The killer came to that room as soon as you'd been watched into your suite. Knocked, and was let in. Just a step or two, and she came out with her news and the suggestion of blackmail. I dare say she'd given him the high sign earlier—plenty of chances down here while he was giving her a light for her cigarette or something. She turned away, and he grabbed up the vase. By its neck. It's a big, heavy thing, that lamp."

"I got it in Italy," said Redfield in his tired voice. "I bought it for an original, but they told me here that I'd been fooled. So I had it made into a lamp, and I put it in that bedroom—where it didn't belong—because the lamp that did belong there got broken."

"Broken? When?"

"Oh, several years ago."

"Did Malcolm know the bronze lamp was there?"

"He may have noticed it. Does a male guest notice such a thing?"

"Slept in that room, has he?"

"Sometimes, when we've had another guest in the room he usually has—the one he has now. When possible I put him in that suite in the north wing with his sister."

Griggs drummed on the mantelshelf. "We'll test the lamp for prints tomorrow, of course, but from what I could see there are none. It was held by the neck, and it could be wiped off in no time. And so we get to the reason why I'm not much interested in Miss Malcolm or Mrs. Drummond, though Mrs. Drummond's a bigger woman. The neck of that lamp is thick, and too short to be swung by both hands. A woman couldn't get a good grasp on it, and I don't think a woman's wrist could swing the lamp at all. I don't think a woman would have thought of using it singlehanded.

"And what's more, if Mrs. Drummond committed the murder she had to cross the room to get the lamp; what excuse would she give for doing that? Well, she might have offered to help fold that spread."

Redfield said: "I shouldn't even have thought of that."

"No, because you're thinking what I'm thinking, Mr. Redfield, whether you'll admit it or not: Malcolm had only to step in from the hall. Mr. Redfield, it's too easy. If Malcolm refused to pay blackmail, do you think his sister would refuse? And if you're wondering how his wife knew about his committing the murder, I can tell you just where she probably stood when he fired the rifle. She stood on the little path that goes down through the woods from the gate behind the tool house. She stood back of that wooden statue and looked through the hedge. I suppose *you* know that the hedge is thin there?"

"Yes," said Johnny. "It's thin there."

"She saw the whole thing. She knew by the way he acted, and by the spot he fired from, that he wasn't shooting at any crow. She may have hung around and heard enough to know that he'd fired at his stepmother and killed her. Anyhow, she saw Malcolm make his getaway, and then came back and got her bike and coasted off—but not far.

"When he kept that appointment with her this evening in her room—it may not have been an appointment, but I think she'd have made one somehow—I don't think he came through his sister's room. I think he came by way of the corridor in the north wing. Why should he tell his sister that he was going to commit another murder? But if he didn't know it himself, and did tell his sister he was going to talk to his wife, we'll never prove it. We might as well give up now and leave Cora Malcolm out. She never swung that vase, and I don't believe that she fired the rifle. It's a man's crime all the way through, and he had the other motive besides—he hated the woman, and he wanted to get rid of her.

"He was tied to her for life. Catch her giving him a divorce now!"

Redfield said: "Griggs, don't you suppose that your argument occurred to him? He's a clever boy. He'd see it all, no matter how wrought up he was. He'd never risk this murder."

"Don't forget that knock on the head he got in France, Mr. Redfield. Don't suppose that that won't be his defense."

"But Griggs, no good lawyer would allow him to plead guilty to homicide—not as things are. We'll all be in for a lot of suspicion. I'm afraid there will be a great deal of irrelevant matter dragged into the evidence by his counsel. That knock on the head will be a last resort, if it's ever used at all. Don't you agree with me, Gamadge?" Redfield looked ready to cry.

"Yes, Johnny, I agree with you."

Griggs smiled grimly. "But considering his motive for the first murder, and considering the fact that he's the one who might have had a double motive for getting rid of his wife, you agree that I'm justified in making an arrest, Mr. Gamadge?"

"I think you're justified. Will you make it tonight?"

"No. I'm going to wait till tomorrow, till I have a chance to talk to Mosson."

"I'd rather like to have a talk with Mr. Malcolm.

He won't talk if he knows he's practically under arrest."

"Everybody's practically under arrest. I won't lock him up in his room, if that's what you mean, but he'll leave his door open, and there'll be a man watching it. I don't suppose he'll try to commit suicide, and I don't suppose he'll murder his sister."

"Commit suicide?" Redfield got up and slowly moved towards the door. "David Malcolm will fight to his last breath."

"You get him a lawyer, Mr. Redfield, and let the lawyer do the fighting."

Redfield went out into the hall, and Griggs turned from the fireplace and crossed to the studio door. He opened it. "All right," he said, "Mr. Drummond."

13

Different Now

Gamadge wondered for a moment after Drummond came in why he seemed like a stranger, then decided that it was because he looked on the point of exhaustion. Gamadge had never seen him even slightly, healthily tired before. After thirty-six holes of golf, or a tremendous climb in the woods, he had always been as fresh as a daisy and ready for anything. He had never been the one to want the evening bridge or poker game broken up, the club dance over.

Now his step dragged, his big shoulders drooped, his face was expressionless, sagging with fatigue. He looked bleakly at Griggs.

"I hope you won't insist on asking my wife any questions tonight, Lieutenant," he said, and there was no truculence in the tone. He spoke slowly, carefully, drearily. "I know this is a very bad situation—"

"Yes," said Griggs, snapping his words off. "It's all different now. No fooling now. Is Mrs. Drummond badly knocked out?"

"She was improving when I left; I found some of that—what do you call it?—spirits of ammonia in the bathroom. But she had a tough experience; terrible shock." He went over to the fire, sat down, and put out his hands to the embers. When Gamadge bent to take a log out of the basket, however, he reacted like the country householder he was: "No, never mind. Don't burn up a fresh log so late—we aren't getting loads of wood in often."

Griggs said: "I have to get her story, Drummond."

"She's told me what happened. Won't that do tonight?"

"What does she say?"

"She'd been getting ready for bed, and she went into the bathroom to draw a hot bath. She saw that Mrs. Malcolm hadn't been before her—no towels had been used, and so on. She wondered if Mrs. Malcolm had what she needed. Knocked, didn't notice that there wasn't any answer, and opened the door. You know what she saw. No wonder she could only stand and scream."

Griggs said: "Kind of her to go in. Kind of her to suggest that Mrs. Malcolm should spend the night here. I wouldn't have said from what went before that she'd bother about Mrs. David Malcolm."

Drummond did not take his eyes from the dying fire. "Didn't care for her, of course," he answered. "But after all there's a routine in these matters, if you've been brought up in a certain way. After Miss Ryder left, my wife was the oldest woman here. As for tonight, there was no maid on duty; and Redfield's better than most men about remembering such things, but after all he's a man. My wife thought Mrs. Malcolm might want something that we"—he shrugged the powerful shoulders—"wouldn't even think of. I don't know whether you're married . . . My wife does her hair up with dozens of gadgets, works like a dog over her face. Redfield wouldn't have stocked up the bathroom with all that."

"I won't ask her any questions till morning, Drummond; but there's a woman coming up from Rivertown to go over her things and Miss Malcolm's things."

"Oh Lord."

"Can't be helped. Now about you."

"I turned right in. I didn't see anything."

"See anything?" Griggs looked at him. "Why should you have seen anything?"

"Thought you knew." Drummond seemed surprised. "There's no bath attached to the room I was moved into when Mrs. David Malcolm decided to stay. I used Johnny's."

"That's so. I forgot that."

"But I wanted to leave it free for him, so I went down the wing the minute I got upstairs. My wife had moved my bag into my new room herself; I just took out some things and went to Johnny's bathroom and came back. Felt as if I'd been in a—felt tired. I pulled off my clothes and got into bed."

"And didn't hear a sound." Griggs supplied this gloomily.

"If I had, I shouldn't have paid any attention."

"You were right across the corridor."

"There are all kinds of sounds at night in the country. You don't pay attention, if you want to sleep. Especially in another man's house, where you don't worry about a loose slate on the roof or a loose shutter."

"But you heard your wife scream."

"That's different."

"Well, just stay in your room for the rest of the night. It's all different now. And our men will be in the house pretty soon, and they won't want people underfoot."

Drummond stood up. "Griggs—"

"Yes, Mr. Drummond?"

"For God's sake, haven't you any evidence about *this* murder?"

"We're getting along."

"I suppose you're pretty well convinced that it's—that it's Malcolm?"

"You leave it to us."

"I mean if it is, it's a psychopathic case. Have they got a man at Rivertown who understands that? If not, Redfield ought to—"

"Just leave it to us, Mr. Drummond."

Drummond glanced vaguely about the room and at Gamadge, put his hands in his coat pockets, took them out again. He went across the room, hesitated at the door, and went out. They heard his heavy step on the stairs.

Griggs looked into the studio. "Miss Malcolm."

She came in; the plum-colored robe was tied tightly about her waist, and she looked as slim and wiry as a boy. She stood waiting while Griggs closed the door.

"Miss Malcolm," he said, "I don't intend to keep you long. First let me remind you that things are different now. I'll ask you to leave your bedroom door ajar. There's a woman coming up, I want you to cooperate; and she'll be looking in on you now and then all night."

"I understand."

"Now just a few questions. Did you leave your room after you went up tonight, until you heard Mrs. Drummond screaming?"

"No."

"Did your brother come through to have a private word with his wife? That would be natural enough."

"He didn't go out of the suite at all."

"But you wouldn't have known it if he'd left for a minute or so by the door into the hall from his bedroom."

"Yes, I should. We were talking."

"All the time?"

"Yes. Most of it through the bathroom, with our doors open. Neither of us was tired. We were wide awake."

Griggs and Miss Malcolm looked at each other calmly enough. At last Griggs said: "If that's the case there's no use in my keeping you any longer or asking you any more questions."

She said: "I was going to tell you that after my brother's wife came this evening, and told us about the bicycle and everything, I thought it was she who had killed Mrs. Archibald Malcolm."

"But you don't think so now?"

"I don't know what to think."

"Miss Malcolm, if you know any earthly reason, except the obvious one, why either of those women should have been murdered, now's the time to come out with it. Don't try to spare anybody's feelings—it's too late for that. Nobody's feelings are going to be spared from now on, and anything you may know might keep some innocent party out of a lot of trouble. Just give me any reason you can think of why either of those women should have been killed."

She said: "Nobody had any motive except my brother and me; we didn't kill them, and all we can think of is that somebody's gone insane."

"Mr. Redfield or Mr. or Mrs. Drummond went insane?"

She was silent.

"Well, I'm sorry you can't help us out," said Griggs in a casual tone. "Neither could Drummond. He suggested a psychiatrist for your brother, though."

Gamadge said: "If your brother should be arrested on the evidence."

After a moment she spoke in a low voice: "What can any of us say?"

"That's right, you're all in a spot. Well, you can go up, Miss Malcolm," said Griggs.

When she had gone Griggs went and summoned the last of his witnesses. Malcolm came in, a slowly moving yellow-and-brown figure with a colorless face. The collar of his yellow pajamas was fastened up around his brown neck, and there was a brown-and-yellow scarf crossed below it. He was smoking.

"No questions, Mr. Malcolm," said Griggs briskly.

"No?"

"What's the use, when your sister has given you an alibi?"

"Very good of you to accept it." The pale lips smiled.

"I might ask you if you know who killed your wife—just for the record."

"I can't imagine who killed her."

"I'll ask you to leave your door open tonight. A man will look in from time to time. He'll look in on the others."

"Like the frontiers, on the sleeping trains in the old days." Malcolm looked at Gamadge. "I wondered whether this gentleman would look in on me before he goes to bed."

Griggs said that it was up to Mr. Gamadge. Gamadge said that he would look in.

Malcolm went at his deliberate pace into the hall, and they heard him say something lightly to the officer there.

Griggs sat down, clasped his hands between his knees, and gazed at the floor. He said: "Redfield's right; those two will fight like tigers. She's going to end up in a bad jam; as an accessory before and after the fact. I couldn't keep her out of it if I wanted to."

"No; you couldn't."

"Wonder what he wants to see you about. Perhaps"—Griggs looked up and grinned—"he wants to hire you."

"Perhaps he does."

"Hire you on spec. He'll have plenty of money if he gets off, and perhaps his sister'd pay you anyhow."

"She might."

"Don't get mad," said Griggs, laughing. "I never heard that you made a practice of getting murders out of trouble."

"I'm not mad," Gamadge assured him benignly. "And a murderess did hire me once."

"You knew she was one?"

"By the time I took the job I knew it, yes. But I had to take the job; she was cooking up evidence against somebody. I had to keep her under my eye. But I didn't," said Gamadge, morosely.

"And you didn't get paid, I suppose."

"No, I didn't."

"Well, you try and get me a nice piece of evidence in this case, something that can be passed around to the jury in a box. Exhibit A, that's all I want; never mind the rest of the alphabet."

Gamadge rose. "I won't get you anything you can hand to the jury in a box. But I'll get you something."

"You will?" Griggs stared.

"If you'll indulge me in my whims."

"What whims?"

"I'll tell you later."

"Why not now?"

"My brain isn't working tonight."

"Just so long as it starts working before the inquests tomorrow afternoon."

"It will."

Griggs was beginning to get a look on his face that Gamadge was used to seeing on the faces of policemen; so Gamadge left him sitting beside the ashes, and went out into the hall and upstairs.

14

Guilty But Insane

Gamadge found Officer Stromer strategically planted in the upper hall; he commanded a view of the main corridor, and could look down the south wing by turning his head; but his eyes were relentlessly fixed on the north wing and Malcolm's doorway.

David Malcolm stood there, leaning against the jamb. Color had returned to his lips, and he was smiling. "Come in, Mr. Gamadge," he said. "We'll sit over there by the windows; then the gendarmerie won't overhear us. I shouldn't like them to."

Cora Malcolm was sitting at a round table there, her elbows on the rosewood surface, her chin on her hands. When Gamadge crossed the room towards her only her eyes moved.

"Have this chair." Malcolm touched the back of one as he passed it, and moved on to another. They sat down.

"Smoke?" Malcolm offered his case.

"I have mine, thanks."

"Cora?"

She took one, and Malcolm lighted hers, Gamadge's, and his own. "I always use one match for three," he said. "A ban always challenges me. Kind of Mr. Gamadge to come in and see us, isn't it, Cora?"

"Kind," she said.

"The truth is, Mr. Gamadge, we read a book of yours in Paris; it was called *Guilty But Insane*. It dealt with problems of the past which have never been officially solved, and why should I tell you that? But perhaps you don't know what a vogue it had with the literary vanguard before the war."

"I heard there were copies sold there. Very gratifying."

"One of our most brilliant friends—you wouldn't have heard of him, before he realized his talents he came to a bad end—called it the Grand Guignol of Elfland."

"I didn't intend to be elfin," said Gamadge, looking somewhat taken aback.

"Elfland can be very macabre. Our friend said that you were the only American he could imagine wanting to know. They didn't think of Cora and me as Americans, you understand; we didn't think of ourselves as belonging to any country. But we found ourselves stirred by some sort of atavistic pride when our doomed friend praised your book. This may sound irrelevant, but it isn't; I have been wondering whether you couldn't help us with our problem; these two murders."

Gamadge said: "Theory doesn't help much, Mr. Malcolm."

"But may I present a theory to you? It's only a theory; we have no evidence that you could offer the police, and I am hoping that you will agree to regard what I say as confidential."

"If it's pure theory, certainly."

"I know of course that I shall be arrested tomorrow; that's certain," continued Malcolm. "I am consulting you on Cora's behalf. I should like to feel that you are watching her interests when I'm not here. But I should tell you first that the situation is slightly complicated—she thinks I committed the murders."

"No, Davy," she said, "I don't."

"Yes, my child, you do." He turned to Gamadge. "She wouldn't have thought so once, no matter what the evidence against me. But she's lost confidence in my moral integrity. There were covenanters among our forebears, Mr. Gamadge, and she has inherited something from them; while I seem to have inherited something from remoter ancestors—the ones that crawled out of caves, you know, carrying stone implements to assault the Roman wall."

"David," she said quietly.

"But although I have done foolish, and worse than foolish things," he went on, ignoring her, "her conviction that I'm a double murderer springs from something more than that. I was operated on"—he put his hand to his head in that automatic gesture—"in the disintegrating French hospital I told you about. And though you can't make a French surgeon of the first class—any surgeon, perhaps—quit his job in the middle by dropping bombs on the roof and breaking the windows of the operating room, you can make him nervous. And afterwards even my wife couldn't get me quite the care—but that's past. The thing is that I still have trouble off and on, and when life at some given moment strikes me as intolerable, I go into what you might call tantrums. I break things."

"No, Davy," said Cora in the same dragging voice, "you don't."

"I broke that alarm clock."

"You knocked it off the table with your elbow. It was an accident."

"I recall a red flash and a tremor of the brain, and then the alarm clock was on the floor. My sister knows all that, Mr. Gamadge, and she also knows how I have always felt about my father's second marriage, and his second wife, and the will."

"I felt as strongly," said Cora.

"No, Cora, you didn't. You never feel as strongly as I do about anything. You never act impulsively. You have had plenty of chances to commit follies, but you haven't taken them.

"And Cora knows, Mr. Gamadge, what it would have meant to me to be able to get rid of my late wife."

He broke off to put out the stub of his cigarette and light another.

"I don't of course wish you," he went on, "to get a worse impression of me than necessary. Freddy was never in love with me, and she wouldn't have objected to a divorce if I had had my father's money to share with her. And I wasn't in love with her, although as a patient I succumbed to her spell. Perhaps you won't believe me, but it was a potent one. And she liked the idea of the marriage, and after all it was the least I could do—to repay her for what she'd done for us. Cora couldn't stand it, though—went on home.

"But Freddy soon got tired of me, and off she went. But she kept an eye on us—couldn't imagine anybody not cheating in money matters if they could. And she was quite justified in thinking that Cora and I might spoil our chance at the extra income that Mrs. Malcolm was offering us; in fact, we had decided—independently—to refuse it. The toadying we might have had to do for ten or twenty years! We preferred to wait until the whole principal came to us in the course of nature; but now Cora thinks I didn't wait.

"And if you deny it, my dear child," he added, looking at her affectionately, "I shall probably go into a tantrum and smash Redfield's nice clock; which"—he glanced up at the mantel—"looks like an antique, and may be of great value."

Cora, her eyes on the cigarette from which she flicked the ash, was silent.

Gamadge said: "You have explained why Miss Malcolm thinks you murdered your stepmother. Why does she think you murdered your wife?"

"I suppose she imagines that Freddy saw me fire that rifle in the rose garden. Or perhaps she thinks I didn't want to pay so much alimony—I can assure you that it would have to be a good deal! Mind you, Cora hasn't said a word of all this; but we are sympathetic mentally, if not morally, and I know what she is thinking.

"Well, that's enough preamble. Now for my theory. You will have to assume for purposes of argument that I didn't commit the murders. My idea is that the person who did commit them has no intention of letting me suffer. Cora was always meant to be the victim. She's to take the blame for the first crime, and then it will be assumed that she committed the second crime to protect herself from blackmail."

"But you are taking the blame for the crimes. What went wrong?"

"Nothing. The evidence against Cora will emerge as if naturally—unless you do something about it."

"Catch the real murderer?" Gamadge regarded him with mild interest.

"Oh, no; you can't catch the party. There'll be no evidence. But I hoped you might scare the party off. Prevent that plot against Cora from ever coming to anything."

"How should I do that?"

"Well, you know these people. I thought you might find some way of putting the fear of God into that particular person."

"But even if I do, your position will remain as it is?"

"Oh, yes. Nothing can be done about my position. I don't want Cora in it, with just the extra bit of evidence that will be fatal for her. I suppose I have some faint chance of getting off?"

"In such cases it usually depends on the judge's summing up and charge to the jury."

"And judges don't like old ladies being killed for money, and they don't like deserted wives being killed by husbands who get tired of them. I suppose that's the way the court would see it. And the story about her saving my life would come out, and the fact that I'm—or was—a man of independent if small income, and she was a working woman. Bad, very bad."

"Something else would come out, Mr. Malcolm; your injury, and it's aftereffects as you describe them. Your lawyer might change the plea. You might get a life sentence, but not of the kind that is shortened by parole."

"Oh yes," said Malcolm. *"Guilty but insane."*

Cora got suddenly to her feet. "I can't stand this," she gasped, and put her hands to her head.

Malcolm sprang up and held her. "I told you not to sit in on it," he said gently. "You'd better go in and lie down. I'll get you some aspirin."

He led her through the bath into her room. After a while he came back, closing the bathroom door after him. He was lighting a cigarette.

"I knew it would be too much for her," he said. "But she has lots of pluck. The unbearable thing for her now, of course, is that she thinks I'm going to try to shove the guilt on somebody else."

"And aren't you?" asked Gamadge.

"Yes; but as I said before, there's no question of turning the party over to the police. That complication doesn't exist to disturb me." He sat down again. "I want to say that if you do pull the thing off, Cora will see that you're paid for your trouble; though no payment could be adequate from my point of view. But I thought ten thousand dollars—"

"Very handsome. But as you remarked before, these people are old friends of mine. I couldn't take money for the job."

"I had to offer it."

"Of course." Gamadge sat up in his chair, pulled the ash tray towards him, stubbed out his cigarette, and went on briskly: "Let's see if we can clarify this idea of yours, which remains obscure to me. You say you know the guilty party. But the field narrows; we have only four suspects left, if we eliminate you and your sister and my cousin Abigail Ryder."

"Miss Ryder? I never dreamed of including her. A charming lady."

"Redfield?"

"I don't know why he should kill his golden goose—my stepmother; but apart from that, he doesn't meet my requirements."

"Drummond?"

"Out. This involves Cora, and he wouldn't hurt a

hair of her head. They think the world of each other—great friends. Though what she sees in him— but that's her business. Perhaps my poor sister has had enough of the mercurial temperament."

"We arrive at Blanche Drummond."

"Unfortunately, we do."

"And why should Blanche Drummond have murdered Mrs. Archibald Malcolm?"

The young man crossed his legs, uncrossed them, put out his cigarette, lighted another, and looked at the ceiling. He said: "I knew this was going to be awkward, and sound like the devil. Perhaps you'll accept my assurance that I wouldn't say a word if it weren't for Cora?"

"Don't apologize, Mr. Malcolm. This is a purely business conversation now."

"Well, the fact is that last summer and the summer before I had a silly affair with Mrs. Drummond. Nothing that really deserves the name of an affair, you know; but it's one of the reasons why Cora has ceased to regard me as a high soul. She likes Drummond, as I said. Well, Mrs. Drummond took the thing seriously. I didn't expect her to. No European of her age would have regarded it as anything but the mildest kind of romantic time-passing. How could I know?"

"We ask that question," murmured Gamadge, "still."

"Cora made me break off this summer. I was for withdrawing gracefully, but she made me speed it up. And Mrs. Drummond knew that Cora was working on it."

"But you are not asking me to think that the murder was a devious attempt at revenge upon your sister?"

"I'm not a fool. I'm afraid Mrs. Drummond did it for the money."

"Let me get this clear. She thought if you had your inheritance, and Cora should afterwards be eliminated from the scene, you would be able to buy your wife off, and make it possible for Blanche to buy Walter off, and marry Blanche?"

"Yes."

"You think that Blanche Drummond staked everything on two divorces and your sister's elimination?"

"She hasn't a realistic point of view."

Gamadge sat back. "I won't comment on that. But during your season of dalliance with Blanche Drummond you must have developed a low opinion of her, Mr. Malcolm. Low indeed."

"I only know that I never in my life heard anybody else talk so much about money, and I never knew anybody to want it so."

"She was brought up to depend on it, and misses it now."

"And she's frightfully annoyed with Drummond for not making it, and for hanging on to that place of theirs next door."

"I accept the theory provisionally. Now as to this evidence that Blanche expects to use against your sister."

"It's been planted—I think."

"What is it?"

"Mr. Gamadge, I shouldn't provide you with evidence against Cora even if I were sure you'd conceal it. I wouldn't trust my own judgment or anybody else's conscience where Cora is concerned. I don't think you *would* conspire to conceal evidence that for all you know mightn't have been planted at all. And

I'm pretty sure that if you speak to Mrs. Drummond, that clue will never be found."

"This rather promises to cramp my style in dealing with Blanche."

"I shouldn't expect everybody to be able to tackle the job."

"She'll draw attention to this thing, whatever it is, before you're taken off to jail?"

"That's what I'm afraid of."

"Well, let's revert to the premise; that she killed your stepmother. No evidence against her, you say."

"None whatever. But think how easily she could have managed it! She told me herself this afternoon, while we were in the orchard, that Miss Ryder had said she was going to take that walk around the Loop. She thought Cora and Drummond were in the flower garden. I was off to the swimming pool. She had her gloves on, she'd just fired the rifle—an excellent shot. Of course she only spent a minute or two in the greenhouse. She came across the road with those pinks—Redfield was out of sight behind his sunflowers."

"What was it she actually said to you while you were hanging up the crows?"

"Suggested going down to the swimming pool—we used to go there. I said what I've been saying all summer—that it wouldn't do."

Gamadge rose, and stood looking down at the young man. "In your position, Mr. Malcolm, if you're innocent, your ancestor with the stone implement would have been laying about him by this time and frothing at the mouth."

"It wouldn't do Cora much good if I frothed at the mouth."

"You seem to have what it takes, anyhow."

Gamadge went out and along the corridor, nodded to Stromer as he passed him, and entered the south wing. He had been wondering how to get a word with Blanche Drummond, but that problem was solved for him. Her door was open a crack and Tilly's eye was applied to the crack.

She whispered: "Meester Gamadge."

"Hello."

"We've been waiting and waiting for you. Meeses Drummond wants to see you."

15

Quite Well

"How is she?" whispered Gamadge.

"Kvite vell now. Poor lady—to find a body!"

"Terrible shock."

"But she is kvite vell now. I go to bed."

"That's right."

Tilly flung the door wide, allowed Gamadge to pass her, and then trotted off. Gamadge stood looking into this most luxurious guest room of the new wing. It was all done in the palest pastel shades of rose, with furniture of some pale wood that glowed in the light like amber. Blanche sat up in the canopied bed, her hands lying on the folded edge of a rosy linen sheet. Long-fingered white hands, large for a woman; but Griggs had not been interested in Blanche Drummond's hands.

Her fair skin looked greenish, and there was blue under her eyes that had not been put there; it gave the eyes a brilliant but a sunken look.

He came over to the bed, drew up a padded chair, and sat down. "Well, Blanche."

"Henry, I want you to telephone Abby Ryder for me the first thing in the morning."

"What do you want me to say to her?"

"I want her to put me up for a few days. I'm not going home. I'm leaving Walter."

Gamadge was silent.

"I'll go to New York as soon as I can," she went on. "I have plenty of friends there."

"What has decided you?"

"Walter hints that I murdered those two women. He doesn't believe it, but that's what he implies."

"He's been fighting tooth and nail for you."

"He wouldn't quite dare to come out with it to the police. But he won't tell them what I say—that that girl committed the murders."

"You seem very sure of it, Blanche."

"Henry, I didn't think *you* were a mush of sentiment."

"But even I require evidence before I make such an assertion as that."

"She was right across the hall from that woman tonight, and she hated her. She hated her a good deal more than David did. And she was up in the tool house this afternoon—she's the one person who *couldn't* have been seen going into the rose garden."

"That's not enough, you know it isn't."

"Evidence always comes out if a person's guilty. There'll *be* evidence—you wait and see."

"She must have known that Mrs. David Malcolm's murder would get her brother into a lot of trouble."

"She thinks they can't do anything to him because there were so many of us. She's really a stupid girl; reserved people often are. It's their way of hiding it. Walter thinks she's wonderful—that type always attracts men like Walter."

"Well," protested Gamadge, "not always. He married you."

"I mean older men. He is perfectly willing to sacrifice me to her. He implies that I could commit murder, and she couldn't."

"He hasn't actually accused you?"

"He asked me why I asked David's wife to stay, and why I went to her room tonight. He asked me why I stayed so long in the greenhouse. I always know what he means, I know him pretty well."

"What motive could he advance for such a theory, Blanche?"

She was silent for a long time; then she said: "Walter thought I was going off with him."

"With David Malcolm?"

"Yes. Of course."

"And were you?"

"How could we, when we shouldn't have had enough money to live decently on?"

"Then why did Walter think you would go?"

"He thought I'd go anyway; we haven't enough money as it is, he will keep up the place here instead of letting it go for taxes. I have to stay up here all spring and summer and autumn because we can't afford New York for more than a few months, and we can't afford to go South. I've wanted a divorce for years. The only reason I didn't insist on one was because I shouldn't have had enough alimony to be comfortable on. Walter was against it because he thought I didn't know my own mind. He wouldn't"—she smiled bitterly—"be against it now."

"And he hints that you murdered Mrs. Archibald Malcolm so David Malcolm should have money to support you on?"

"Yes. But he doesn't dare come out with it—hint it to the police—because that girl would marry him tomorrow if she could, and he's insane about her, and he wouldn't like me to come out with *that!*"

"He's protecting Miss Malcolm and himself?"

After a long pause she said: "Yes."

"But without further evidence it might be fair to assume that you are protecting yourself and David Malcolm?"

Blanche did not look at him. She said: "I'm sure there'll be evidence."

"There's a little now, Blanche; but not against Walter. Let me assure you that I was staggered when I came back tonight and found that it was you who had persuaded Mrs. David Malcolm to stay."

A sudden commotion in the house, doors closing, voices, feet on the stairs, caused her to turn her head on the pillow and look at the half-open door. At last she spoke again: "Cora suggested it first."

"But Malcolm's wife turned that suggestion down. Why did you get her to stay, Blanche? Why did you go into her room afterwards?"

"I was sorry for the poor creature."

"No, you weren't. Griggs may swallow that theory, though even he chokes on it; but he doesn't know you well enough to *know* that it's false. Didn't you want her to stay so that you could find out whether she'd give Malcolm a divorce now that he was going to have money? She was probably waiting for big alimony too, you know. You'd understand all about that."

Blanche met his eyes. "It wasn't just the money. I wanted him to be free. She'd taken a frightful advantage of him—poor, inexperienced, unworldly boy! Not that I ought to call him a boy; he's mature intellectually. He never was young, except in experience. But he's incapable of killing anybody for money."

"Does Walter say she told you she preferred to stay married to Malcolm, and that you solved the problem by murder, and then waited and pretended to find her body afterwards?"

"Henry, you don't think that."

Gamadge, knowing what Malcolm thought, or at least said he thought, felt in spite of himself a grudging pity. "Whatever you do, Blanche, or whatever happens," he said, "don't count on Malcolm. He's too young. He was always too young. You've pursued a shadow."

But her expression told him that it was useless to argue with a human being obsessed. He rose, went out into the corridor, and shut the door behind him.

Griggs was in the center of a crowd that thronged the main hall. Gamadge joined it, pushed through, and seized the lieutenant by the elbow. "Griggs—come along here a minute. I want to speak to you."

Griggs looked at him as if they had never met before, then he allowed himself to be urged into the quiet of the north wing. "Well?" he asked.

"Tomorrow morning I want to take the whole lot of them down to the rose garden."

"Take who?"

"Drummonds, Redfield, Malcolms. Conference on the scene of the first crime."

Griggs laughed shortly. "I'd like to see you stampede one of this gang."

"But you mustn't see me. I won't get any results if there's a policeman within earshot of the place."

"Results! I don't believe in that kind of charade."

"I've had a little luck—"

"Yes, I know the kind of luck you have. But I oughtn't to turn Malcolm loose like that."

"Loose! What do you mean, 'loose'? You can post officers all over the grounds. The garden's an enclosure."

Griggs reflected, frowning. Then he asked: "What did Malcolm want to see you about?"

"Wants me to look after his sister for him."

"Cool. Why didn't he ask Redfield?"

"Business matter. He offered me compensation."

"How much?" Griggs was interested.

"Ten thousand dollars."

"Ten thou . . ." Griggs' voice faded.

"But I won't get it," explained Gamadge.

"You won't?"

"I didn't accept the job." As Griggs stared, he went on: "Will you send them down to the rose garden tomorrow early, as soon as they've had breakfast? I think I really could get something for you."

"Ask me in the morning. I'll see."

"Thanks." Gamadge went back to the south wing, and opened the door of Redfield's suite. A light burned in the study, the day bed was prepared, and no sound came from the room beyond the bath. But if Redfield slept, Gamadge didn't until dawn.

16

Secrets of the Heart

Gamadge sat down alone to breakfast in the dining room. Alice, waiting on him in the intervals of laying trays, which Tilly afterwards pattered away with, looked aloof and oppressed. Gamadge dared not imagine Mrs. Debenham's reaction this morning to the news of the second murder, nor could he bear to contemplate the interpretation that would have been put on it in the Islands.

There was a great coming and going of cars in the drive—the Law and the Press. Mosson looked in on him, made a face, lifted his shoulders, said nothing, and went away.

When the clock struck nine Gamadge sought the nearest telephone. He got a party in New York, talked for three minutes, said: "Thanks, Tommy," and put the receiver back. He went out of the house by way of the terrace.

Griggs accosted him there, looking as though his night on the studio couch had not agreed with him. But he said: "Go to it. Have your damn silly experiment."

"Lieutenant, this is good of you."

"It's foolish of *you*. I'd like it better if one of my men could be listening."

"I'll call the whole thing off if I see anybody within earshot."

"There's the sheriff's deputy down in the lower garden, and a man up by the tool house, and one in the rockery with a good view of the entrance to the place, and one outside that gate. But the whole enclosure is nothing but a series of exits."

"Nobody's going to exit unless I say so."

"That's talking!" Griggs was amused.

"Who's rounding the crowd up?"

"Redfield. He had a little trouble with Mrs. Drummond—she was thinking of spending the morning in bed. But he got her going, and they'll be down there in ten minutes."

Gamadge walked down to the rockery. He found an officer sitting under the birch at the lower pool, in silent communion with a frog. The frog sat on the pool wall, breathing heavily.

The officer said: "I thought at first it wasn't real."

"You have to throw a twig to find out."

"I kind of hated to lose him."

"I think he's an old friend of mine. He distracted my attention badly once, not so long ago."

"He won't distract mine." The officer looked in front of him, down to the lawn and across it. "I'll move when they get into that place. Watch the whole front."

Gamadge, avoiding the frog's side of the pool, went on down. The lawn lay fresh and bright in warm sunshine, crickets had begun their song. When he entered the rose garden he found that a wet and pinkish rose had come out in a corner bed.

"And thou must die," he informed it. He felt sad and sententious.

Drummond came in, strolling as if on a tour of casual inspection. He had acquired his pipe, and was smoking it. He wandered over to look at the rose, said nothing to Gamadge, and wandered on.

Johnny Redfield came in, his hand under Blanche Drummond's arm. She had a waxy look, but was turned out with all her accustomed finish.

Redfield said: "Not a bad idea of yours, Gamadge, a conference. Gives us an airing, anyway."

Blanche looked at Gamadge. "Henry, did you telephone to Abigail as I asked you?"

"Not yet, Blanche. Plenty of time."

"No reason on earth you shouldn't stay with me." Redfield looked at Drummond's back, and lowered his voice. "No reason at all. No reason you shouldn't go home, if it comes to that. Gamadge, this poor girl is quite mistaken about everything. Everything."

Blanche said: "Why, here's a rose! Johnny, what's it's name? Ours are still coming out, too."

"I never can tell those pink ones apart," said Redfield. "Even George couldn't teach me."

The Malcolms appeared, Malcolm's arm through his sister's, his hand lightly covering hers.

He stood looking at Gamadge, and his expression was that of one who finds a problem insoluble. Then he said, a faint contempt in his voice: "Cora and I are being—what's the phrase?—'pushed around,' Mr. Gamadge. Otherwise we shouldn't have joined your conference."

"I thought you would have guessed—I thought all of you would have guessed that it's not a conference."

"Not?"

"No. We're here for another purpose, and one so private that I have Griggs word for it we're not to be listened in on. But for our own comfort let's make sure that we shan't be." Gamadge surveyed the enclosure. "There is a bench in every corner, and the outside world can be seen by turning and parting the vines. Blanche, will you sit there—to the left of the entrance?"

She looked at him, vaguely, and then walked over to the rustic seat and sank down on it.

"Redfield, will you sit there on my left? And Drummond on my right? And I'll stand here beside Apollo, where I can see you all."

Redfield went slowly to his appointed place; his puzzled eyes fixed on Gamadge as if imploringly. Drummond stood where he was.

"To keep a lookout, Walter," said Gamadge politely. "Would you mind very much?"

Drummond backed into the corner; but he did not sit down.

"And you and your sister, Mr. Malcolm; may I ask you to occupy the remaining point of the compass?"

Cora put her left hand on her brother's left, turned him, and gently urged him over to the bench indicated. It was just beyond the pile of turfs, and placed like the others, across the corner. She sat down; Malcolm slowly settled himself at her feet.

"Thank you," said Gamadge. "Now for our purpose in being here. Surely you know that it's to look for Miss Malcolm's gold pin?"

Redfield said hoarsely: "Gamadge—for heaven's sake . . ."

"Surely"—Gamadge turned his head to look at him—"it will be best for us to find it before the police do? Of course they never may; they don't know that there is such a thing as that gold heart, much less that it was lost. Nobody's mentioned its loss to them; nobody's spoken of it at all since Blanche Drummond spoke of it just outside this place yesterday afternoon. Called our attention to the fact that Miss Malcolm had lost it—you remember?"

He turned his eyes to Drummond, then to the Malcolms, then to Blanche. Redfield said: "Gamadge, I don't know what you're talking about. I had no idea it was lost."

"You didn't hear Blanche speak of it; that's quite true, Johnny," said Gamadge. "You came through the gate just afterwards. But Miss Malcolm was facing the rose garden—she had been about to go in when I stopped her. She was therefore facing you, or nearly so, as you came towards us; you, of all people would notice that the pin had gone from her lapel. It's the kind of thing you wouldn't miss. It was no ordinary pin, you know; it was large, it was a curio, it was very noticeable; and it was a gift from the murdered woman.

"The murder was sprung on us just afterwards. It would drive a trifle of that kind from our heads!"

"Would it? But we'll return to that question. I'll go back now to my remark that the police haven't found it; not the proper word, since they don't know it exists; they haven't looked for it. What I should have said was that they didn't see it when they were going over that corner where the dislodged turf is, and where the rifle and the gloves were. I didn't see it either, when I looked the spot over myself—just after the crime. But I *might* have missed it; they wouldn't. It isn't there.

"Where is it, then? Somewhere, I suppose, on Miss Malcolm's route across the garden from the west side to that corner. I propose to search for it along that route."

"But Gamadge—" Johnny almost shouted it, and then, with a glance at the green wall behind him, lowered his voice. "Why do you imagine it *is* here? What earthly reason—"

Gamadge said: "Perhaps it would be best to tell you now. We return to your first objection—that the loss of the pin would have been driven from your heads by my announcement that there had been a murder.

"I say it wouldn't. I say it would have been fixed in your minds after that announcement, by the very fact that there had been a murder. I, of course, knowing beforehand about the murder, noticed everything. I saw that the pin was gone from Miss Malcolm's coat, and I prevented her from entering this place. I heard Blanche call attention to the loss of the pin.

"I noted the following facts:

"You never mentioned the lost pin at all, then or later—although it was the dead woman's gift to Miss Malcolm, a 'token'; although you are interested in everything, even trifles, that affects the happiness of your guests. Happiness? Anything that affects them at all affects you as a host. Normally, I swear that you would have kept after the police and the deputy and the rest of them until that pin had been looked for with torches and floodlights.

"You never spoke of it even to me.

"Blanche Drummond called our attention to the loss, and then she never spoke of it again.

"Drummond never mentioned it either; you'd think he would have said whether Miss Malcolm was wearing it when she was with him in the lower garden. I have ventured to guess that he hasn't mentioned it precisely because she did have it on when she left him there."

Drummond stood, pipe in hand, gazing at nothing.

"Miss Malcolm hasn't referred to it," continued Gamadge. "I gave her a lead last night, but she didn't follow it. Malcolm"—he met the young man's stony look—"hasn't named it.

"My cousin Abigail may I think be excepted from this roster; she came late upon the scene yesterday afternoon, Miss Malcolm wasn't facing in her direction by that time, and she didn't hear Blanche Drummond's announcement. But perhaps even she can't be excepted. However: to my conclusion—subject, of course to disproof: though the loss of the pin wasn't referred to again, it hadn't been forgotten. Nobody dared mention it.

"Why not? I thought there could be only one answer to that question: all but one of you thought it was here.

"And that one knew it was here."

Crickets sang in the warm, bright, sheltered place. There was no other sound until Blanche Drummond cried: "Why, Henry, what do you mean?"

"I'll tell you how I bolstered up the theory. But even before I looked for evidence to bolster it—negative evidence—I made sure that if the pin were here it shouldn't be removed; if it were not, that it shouldn't be planted. The rose garden was under my eye almost from the time the murderer left it until the state policeman came. Nobody had entered, I didn't enter it again. I didn't want anybody, certainly not the police, to see me looking about in here; I had no wish to give them ideas that there was something to be looked for.

"One of you might have come back, and I didn't want any of *you* to see me looking, either."

Drummond asked roughly: "Why the devil not?"

"Well, Walter, perhaps someone wanted it found. So that they could tell the police, explaining that they hadn't found it themselves."

Blanche said: "But *Henry* . . . !"

"I needed certain evidence," continued Gamadge, "that my theories were correct. As soon as the state policeman came I acted. I followed Miss Malcolm's footsteps along the way she said she had come from the lower garden; but I also followed the route she might have taken from the tool house down here. I tried to behave as if I were simply strolling. The light wasn't too good, but as I keep reminding you, the pin is large and bright. It would show up against grass, earth, or dead leaves.

"I went up from the west side of this enclosure to the tool house; I went into the tool house and looked into the croquet box—Miss Malcolm had bent over it when she took out her mallet. I walked through into the woods, and down to the Loop. I went into the flower garden, searched behind the cosmos, came back the other way. I retraced my steps to the tool house.

"No pin. Though the search was far from conclusive, I was pretty well convinced that only two theories were tenable; she had dropped it in the rose garden, or somebody else had picked it up outside.

"But why should that person not have said so?"

There was another silence.

"I think I'm justified in looking for it here," continued Gamadge. "Before I do so, however, I should like to explain why I don't think Miss Malcolm is the one who dropped it here."

Drummond moved a few steps backward, looked behind him at the rustic bench, and sat slowly down on it. Cora Malcolm's face did not change; her brother's seemed actually to dissolve from a masklike rigidity into the warmth and texture of humanity.

"Miss Malcolm," said Gamadge, "did try to enter this place yesterday when she came down from the tool house. But she had expressed a wish to see the Apollo; and if she had wanted to look for the pin here, she would have come through the upper side of the place, through the vines. We shouldn't have seen or heard her.

"And although Blanche described her as looking terrified, I thought she looked not terrified but depressed."

He straightened, took his hands out of his pockets, and went on more briskly: "Well: shall I, as the disinterested observer, hunt for this object? You must all watch me; but I promise you I shan't palm it!"

Redfield muttered: "*I* should."

"I believe you would, Johnny."

Gamadge walked over to the Malcolm's corner. From there he came back across the garden, following the turfed paths, bending to brush aside uncut grass from the edges of the rose beds. It was not until he had arrived at a bed nearly halfway along the west trellis, and moved a clump of encroaching chickweed, that he stood up with the gold heart glittering in his fingers.

"Not hard to find," he said, "if you looked."

Blanche said: "I knew it would be here! I knew it

192   *Elizabeth Daly*

would be here! Right where she would have come in
from the tool house! And here it is!"

"Yes. Here it is, Blanche. Now let me discourse
upon it a little," said Gamadge, walking back to his
station beside the Apollo. "For of course, (I quite
agree with you, Blanche), I required more than these
flimsy conjectures to persuade me that Miss Malcolm
wasn't a criminal. Miss Malcolm has been calm; but
I've known murderers who were calmer. No: if she
wasn't at any time my favorite suspect, it was because
of the pin itself. It has argued her case for her, and
for me.

"I have a way of letting things speak for themselves. I have followed this course when the thing was
a book; when the thing was a picture. I followed it
when—but doesn't any of you really know what this
thing is?"

The sunlight glittered on the gold heart. Redfield
said: "We all know what it is."

"None of you does. I can see that in your faces. But
I knew what it was the moment I had it in my hand
at the cocktail party yesterday, and this morning—to
be quite certain—I called up a friend in the antique
jewelry business and got his verdict. I'd never seen
one like it, but I've seen another piece of jewelry
with—let me say—the same meaning. It's a rebus."

Gamadge looked about him at blank faces.

"When Miss Malcolm received it," he went on,
"she thought it a paltry gift. Perhaps the giver meant
it to be one. But as a matter of fact, it's rather rare.
Five little colored stones, and a diamond in the
middle; an odd and rather awkward arrangement of
jewels; three different-colored red ones, two of them
in a row. Miss Malcolm didn't call them off in the

proper order, and she thought the paler ruby was a tourmaline. But say it like this: Ruby, Emerald, Garnet, Amythyst, Ruby, Diamond. What does that spell? Has none of you heard of a Regard *ring?*"

Drummond gave an exclamation. "My mother had one—it was her grandmother's." He added: "I liked to look at it when I was a kid—read off the row of stones. But I hardly noticed the thing yesterday, and the stones aren't in a row, and the diamond's in the middle."

"That makes it harder," agreed Gamadge. "I nearly missed it myself. But my grand-aunt used to let *me* read off *Regard* on her ring, and I did happen to notice that the right stones were all on this pin. I'd never seen a Regard pin before, and I was amused. Such a mass of sentiment it is, three times as sentimental as a ring! There's the heart shape to begin with, and then the locket with the hair. When it was presented to Miss Malcolm yesterday, and the giver called it a 'token,' I nearly added: 'A token of regard.'"

"Well," asked Drummond, "and why didn't you?"

"Do you remember the circumstances, Walter? The situation was strained; the ladies seemed to feel a good deal less than regard for each other. My remark might have produced an ironical comment from Miss Malcolm. I'm all for peace; I decided to let the episode pass, and to acquaint Miss Malcolm with the pin's secret at some safer moment."

"But Mrs. Malcolm talked about a secret," said Blanche irritably. "She said it was that concealed locket in the back of the pin."

"Which is no secret at all. She pointed out a secret, but she didn't know what the real secret was. Well, it

wasn't surprising that she didn't; Mr. Archibald Malcolm mightn't have known it himself—a man doesn't
always know unimportant things about unimportant
pieces of old family jewelry. But she said there was *a*
secret, and mentioned the wrong one."

"Funny," said Redfield.

"But not funny enough to impress me at the time,"
said Gamadge. "I'm not pretending that this ornament gave me the name of the murderer. I'm only saying that after I had formulated my theory, the Regard
pin helped to strengthen it."

Blanche gave a high, tremulous laugh. "Why
Henry," she said again, "what *do* you *mean?*"

17

Special Session

Gamadge said: "I mean that that having cleared the danger to Miss Malcolm out of the way—think what it would have meant if the police had found this and had asked questions!—we may now proceed to the main business of this meeting. You all realize that the murderer is with us here. Shall we—or rather will you—hold a court of your own? I must prosecute, but you are judge and jury. The defendant will offer us what extenuating circumstances there may be. You will then decide whether to call in the police and hand the accused over to justice, or to act in another way that I shall suggest."

"An escape could be managed?" inquired Malcolm, looking about him with a smile.

"We haven't reached that stage of the proceedings, Mr. Malcolm."

Drummond got up again. "Are we to take your word for it?" he asked. "About who's guilty?"

"I only intend to present you with the evidence, Walter. You must act on it as you see fit."

"I'm wondering about the possibilities of a flight," insisted Malcolm. "There's a policeman behind every bush."

"Leave that to me, and let us get the trial over

with. I open the case for the prosecution by reminding you that the accused is one of us; not an habitual criminal, therefore, but on the other hand not excusable on the score of having lacked privileges, education, and the teachings of tradition and civilized life.

"And though the accused may have acted twice under some dreadful provocation, perhaps even without premeditation in either case, we must offset that by the fact that this pin was planted here for one base purpose—to incriminate Miss Malcolm. Miss Malcolm had a very strong motive for doing away with her stepmother, she had the means and the opportunity for both crimes. This piece of evidence in my hand would certainly have turned the scale and condemned her to death.

"And this piece of evidence was meant to be found. If the police hadn't found it some hint would have sent them looking for it. The murderer, of course, couldn't find it or hint too strongly—that might suggest a plant, and that would be fatal to the person who had arranged the plant. Well, I've opened for the prosecution. We'll waive formalities. Anybody want to say anything now before I go on?"

Drummond said: "Gamadge—about the frame-up."

"Yes, Walter?"

He cleared his throat. "I'm a lawyer; if I were speaking for the defense I'd make a suggestion here."

"Let's have it."

"Suppose the accused picked that pin up, as you said, on the road outside or somewhere. Wherever Cora dropped it. Stuck it in a lapel, say, as one does, meaning to return it. Then came in here to do the shooting, and it fell—where you found it; the party may have started by running that way, and then remembered that C—Miss Malcolm was up there.

"It would be an awful temptation afterwards— when the party realized it had been dropped—to say nothing and hope it wouldn't be found. I mean the frame-up mightn't have been premeditated, and for all we know the thing *wouldn't* have been found. The party may have meant to come back as soon as possible and get it. Nobody's had a chance yet. This is the first time anybody's been allowed to set foot here."

"So it is. There's a slight element of coincidence in two people's dropping the thing—"

Cora said: "The catch is loose. I mean there is no safety catch."

"Cora can't believe in the frame-up yet," said her brother. "She never believed the pin would be found here."

"Well, we must make a note of Drummond's point. Anybody else wish to say anything? No. Then we'll proceed," said Gamadge, and balanced the gold heart on his palm.

"It was not until eight o'clock last night that I had a case, or the makings of one; but from the first the sun worshiper had interested me very much. She had puzzled me very much. In the first place, why was she a sun worshiper at all? She was supposed to have been a devotee of astrology, and she had kept her astral name. I had never heard of anyone deserting a pseudo-science like astrology for something even more remote from reason. Astrology is hedged in and defined by rules and calculations, its followers consider it a true science, and are guided in their daily lives and most important decisions by its forecasts and its warnings.

"But a sun cult? For all I know, ancient mysteries

may have been revived and practiced in Southern California, esoteric rites connected with the worship of Apollo may be performed there; but it would be a very different thing from astrology to live by. And this sun worshiper talked of it vaguely, not to say flightily, and—what particularly interested me—dressed for it sketchily.

"One might have accepted any kind of pseudo-classical outfit, or even the sort of shapeless affair, on the lines of the djibbah, which would remind one of the worship of Ra, if not of Phoebus Apollo. One would at any rate have expected a definite costume, premeditated and designed. Vega's costume was quite obviously a house robe or tea gown—worn at ankle length, by the way, a length I was not familiar with in such garments; they always in my experience reach the floor. She wore with it a cord from a dressing gown or bathrobe, which assorted ill with the rich materials of the tea gown; modern and fashionable sandals for beach or country wear; and a wreath.

"Last night I went up to her room and examined her wardrobe. The cord had been taken from a bathgown, as I thought. The wreath had been removed from a summer hat. The yellow garment was one of three similar costumes, of similar length.

"There was an effect here of improvisation. But there was another implication too, one far more sinister than that of a hastily assembled costume for the rôle of sun worshiper. Apart from the loose, ankle-length tea gowns there was a complete wardrobe of conservative clothing, normally cut for a woman of her height and build, with hats and shoes to match.

"I will add another fact. When I first entered the room I found Mrs. David Malcolm there; she had come into the house unannounced, and was looking for her husband's room; she was going to wait for him there, and have a word with him in private. We exchanged a few words, and then she asked me who the dead woman was.

"But she knew that Mrs. Archibald Malcolm had been staying at Idlers, she knew that Mrs. Archibald Malcolm was an elderly lady. Why didn't she ask: 'Can this be Mrs. Malcolm, my husband's stepmother, through whose death he would inherit a lot of money?' The matter was of burning interest to her, but she asked nothing of the kind.

"And when I said that it was Mrs. Archibald Malcolm's body, and she looked at the dead face, her own expressed nothing—nothing—but a vast astonishment.

"To sum up my conclusions:

"The 'sun cult' had been invented by Vega after her arrival at Idlers, perhaps after she had seen the figure of Apollo—if such it be. She built up her invention with the help of garments that hung in her wardrobe.

"But there were two distinct sets of these garments; one set, plain and conservative, with all its accessories of hats and shoes, made and cut to fit a tall thin woman; the other set consisting only of three tea gowns, with matching sandals. These might have belonged to a shorter, stouter woman, with shorter feet; a woman of lively and luxurious tastes, and the means to gratify them. They, and the sandals, and the undergarments in the dresser, were the only articles from such a woman's wardrobe that 'Vega' could possibly have worn; their looseness could be tied in with the cord, their shortness would not be as conspicuous as the shortness of a dress, and of course the sandals were heelless and toeless.

"Looking at the things in the top drawer of the dresser, I thought again of the Regard pin. It had been bought for reasons of sentiment—because it *was* a Regard pin; and therefore its secret and the history of its purchase were intertwined. Mrs. Archibald Malcolm might have known neither; but if she knew one she must have known both. That sort of detail goes together.

"But 'Vega,' although she pretended to know the details and circumstances of its purchase, didn't know the secret of the pin, a secret inherent in the arrangement of the colored stones and the little diamond. I concluded that she therefore didn't know its history either, and that all her talk about the pin was pure invention, the kind of invention that is always used by an imposter, if there is no likelihood of contradiction, to show intimate knowledge of the family which the impostor claims to belong to. The young Malcolms evidently knew nothing about the pin; they knew no more about it than the impostor did.

"But it was through no fault of hers that I finally became convinced of her imposture. I became convinced of it when Mrs. David Malcolm showed amazement, nothing but amazement, at my announcement that the dead body was Mrs. Archibald Malcolm's. She showed amazement—quickly suppressed—because she knew it wasn't. At some time, and without the knowledge of David Malcolm, his sister, or Redfield, she had seen, perhaps had met, Mrs. Archibald Malcolm. It would have been like her to make the contact privately, for her own satisfaction.

"I realized at once that she was going to keep her

astounding discovery to herself; and I could only think that she intended to use it for purposes of extortion or blackmail. I should never have left Idlers that night, and chanced the second murder, if I had not believed that she was leaving it too; and I had been told by Griggs that she would be under guard on her journey to Old Bridge and all last night.

"For she could only have blackmailed the one other person at Idlers who had known Mrs. Archibald Malcolm, and that person had committed murder as well as fraud, and might kill again in self defense. I might even, as it was, have been in time to prevent it, but Mrs. David Malcolm was a woman of action and had wasted not a moment in opening her campaign. Nor had her victim lost a moment before silencing her forever.

"I think the Drummonds, I think even the Malcolms will forgive me for leaving them in a state of anxiety—to put it mildly—for twelve hours. Miss Malcolm's pin was in this garden, and couldn't be found—without rousing the interest of the police—until daylight; and even by daylight I had to have an excuse for looking for it without police attendance. If they had known that it was here, no later explanation of mine might have sufficed to keep Miss Malcolm out of the case and out of the papers; and we all know that once a name is bracketed with evidence in a murder case, there will always be people to argue that the owner of the name belongs in the murder case; there are always people who can't be persuaded to forget that name; they 'don't care what you say.'

"Moreover, I hadn't any theory until after eight o'clock last night—late for getting proofs of identification from Pasadena and the bank in Los Angeles. I wanted available proof before making my accusation, even to you; and I wanted my chance to hold this private court. So, I think, would you have wanted it, for we all liked Redfield.

"Well, Johnny." Gamadge turned to look at him. "You were the only one of us who knew Mrs. Archibald Malcolm. You were the only one of us who might have had a legitimate errand here yesterday afternoon—if you didn't need the gardening gloves or the weeding spud, you certainly needed the basket; yours was much too full of marigolds. We know where Miss Gouch is, she's up at Idlers waiting to be viewed by a coroner's jury. But you must tell us where you buried Mrs. Malcolm."

David Malcolm sprang to his feet, and swung to look at the piled squares of turf behind him. "Not there?" He swung back again to look at Gamadge. "Not there! The ground beneath hasn't been dug."

"No," said Gamadge, "not there. And not"—he put out his hand and sent the wooden image rocking—"not here. The base of this thing doesn't cover a foot of turf, and the grass hasn't been disturbed. Well, Johnny." He turned once more to Redfield, who sat with his hands hanging between his knees, his head lowered and his eyes half closed. "Aren't you going to help us? Must I explain to your friends that it made no sort of difference whether this thing was Apollo, or Orpheus, or only a fancy figure off a bandwagon? It could have been of any shape or form, couldn't it, so long as it had a back, and its back was turned to the woods? For who looks for a grave behind its monument?"

Redfield gestured vaguely with both hands; he did not raise his eyes.

"I know," said Gamadge. "You don't want to look at it. But it was an ingenious arrangement; who disturbs underbrush when props are sunk in it—props to support a statue? Not your old occasional man, not the Wilson boy. Your gardener George would have been more inquisitive; you couldn't have risked the arrangement if he'd been here—he would have been sure to clear the underbrush away to see if the props were secure. What would he have uncovered? The lid of the old watering trough? Abby told me it was somewhere in this neighborhood. It would be wide and deep. It would hold Mrs. Malcolm's body, and the rest of her clothes, and all Miss Gouch's luggage."

Blanche Drummond covered her eyes. She gasped: "I can't bear it!"

"But we need you, Blanche," said Gamadge. "You're one of the jury."

Redfield lifted his head at last. "I didn't kill *her*, Blanche. I didn't plant Cora's pin." He looked at Drummond. "It was just as you said, Walter. I was half out of my wits afterwards, and I ran for this side of the trellis. Then I remembered that Cora was up at the tool house, and I turned and ran the other way. But I had got half way through the vines, and something—a tendril—must have caught the thing. I never realized I didn't have it until I saw that it wasn't on Cora, and remembered."

Drummond said harshly: "You left it here to be found, Redfield."

"I didn't think they'd find it. I hoped they wouldn't. They didn't find it, Walter. Since last night I've been—my God, none of you understands. I'll tell you what happened. I'll explain."

18

Civilized

Redfield seemed to pull himself together. He sat up, felt in his pockets, and got out matches and his cigarette case. By the time he had lighted a cigarette his mood had altered; he watched the smoke rise on the still air, and his face hardened. By the time he began to speak his tone was ironical and cold:

"If I'm to defend myself I'd better do a good job. Get it all in, say everything; nobody'll say it for me.

"It's all very well for Gamadge to talk about being civilized and having traditions. If you're civilized, that means you're used to the decencies of life and can't get along without them. Your traditions clamp you to those decencies; nobody becomes civilized in a minute. I wish anybody here could have been in my jam; I wonder what any of you would have done? I'm not so sure you wouldn't have behaved as I did.

"Take Gamadge. He has enough to be comfortable on without working—he's proved it. He doesn't do a thing but volunteer war work now, and he married a girl with some money of her own and more coming. I'd like to try him out in a fix like mine.

"Take Walter Drummond. Walter's as fond of his place up here as I am of mine; he's martyrized Blanche for years so that he can hang on to it. If he'd do that—and he was fond of Blanche once, too—what would he have done if he'd been up against my problem?

"And what has all that done to Blanche? What have her traditions done to her? She thinks of practically nothing but keeping up in the old style, and she thinks it's a crime to deprive her of a new hat. Well, never mind; I'm fond of Blanche, and I'm sorry for her.

"Then look at the Malcolm children. They're good children, I was always fond of them; but I saw their faults. They were brought up to think they'd always be rich, and spoiled by their mother. And when their money was taken away from them—only temporarily, mind! They didn't have to worry about *their* old age—what did they do? Set up as a couple of Hamlets; The Dispossessed! Lived on their incomes—and very well, too, in Paris—and on their expectations. Never even tried to earn. So civilized, you know. But they were willing to make friends with my poor aunt when they found they hadn't enough money to be comfortable over here. They wouldn't kill for money, I suppose, but neither did I.

"But she never offered *me* an income! No indeed. That five thousand wasn't a present, you know—the five thousand she sent me every year. She wanted to buy the children, but she didn't have to buy me. I was going to get her money when she died, if she had any saved then. I didn't think she'd have much. Meanwhile I was to invest the five thousand for her.

"I didn't invest it, I spent it; and whoever tells you that five thousand doesn't make a difference in keeping up a place like Idlers—he's a liar, that's all. I couldn't have kept Idlers going without it. I never had the slightest fear she'd find out I was spending it; she hated business, and she trusted me, and she never asked for an accounting or a receipt. And I simply looked at it as part of my own future inheritance—my own. What was the difference, since I paid her a fair income—four and a half per cent?

"Only of late years, when the percentage began to mount up from the accumulated capital she'd sent me, I persuaded her to let me invest the income too. I was her residuary legatee, and would have had access to all her papers, and every spring I made sure all over again that she wasn't keeping memoranda. There was nothing to connect me with the money except her checks, which were her own business, and nothing to prove that the five thousand a year wasn't a present. I never even worried about it.

"Besides, she wasn't a good insurance risk. She hated doctors, but one of her other companions told me once that she had high blood pressure. And last spring Gouch said she was sure Aunt had had a slight stroke.

"I never liked Gouch. Officious, talky, always writing me about Aunt's health and Aunt's feelings. Lately it was pure hypocrisy. She'd been getting my aunt all worked up about the capital I had had from her, and the income I was keeping back, and the accounts I never sent in. And I thought she was just one of Aunt's reduced gentlewomen, not slated to last!

"I didn't realize, of course, that Aunt was by that time all wrapped up in the stars. She'd turned all her business over to the creature, and Gouch knew her income and expenditures. And Gouch finally convinced her that she'd better pay me a visit—without saying she was bringing Gouch along—to get details.

"You know I drive the station wagon myself this summer. When I saw that woman get off the train with Aunt, and saw poor Aunt's expression when we met, I knew something was up. I ought to have known beforehand that there was something queer about her coming at all. She said she wanted to see the old place before she died, but she never liked it. She wasn't happy here as a girl.

"We got into the station wagon, those two behind with the luggage. Gouch only had a couple of bags. Aunt Josie couldn't wait; she began to talk about the money, and an accounting, and of having brought a statement with her (only Gouch had it) and so on. I wondered what to do. If Gouch hadn't been along it would have been easy enough to manage, but you ought to have heard *her* putting her oar in! By the time we were in the lane here we were in a brawl. Suddenly Gouch screamed. I braked the car. By the time I got around to the back, Aunt was dead.

"I was going to jump back in and drive up to the house; but that was when Gouch took charge. She stood there in the road and said I didn't quite understand the situation. Her brain was working like an engine, and like a fool I let it work; I talked away as airily as you please. I reminded her that I was Aunt's sole heir, and her executor, and I told her she could go to the devil. Nobody would pay any attention to what she said, and we'd just forget the whole thing. I'd give her a nice little present, and I'd get poor Aunt up to the house and get hold of the doctor, and then Alice would drive Gouch back to Rivertown to catch the half-past eight to New York. With Aunt Josie dead she couldn't touch me.

"Gouch said that was all I knew about it. Aunt had made a new will, lodged at the bank, and there was a copy of it in her bag. She was leaving one-fifth of her property to an astrological society, and they'd be very much interested in the difference between what the tax people would find in Los Angeles and the five thousand a year and income I'd been having for years. It might double the estate. I hadn't been stealing from my own future inheritance, I'd been stealing from the United Brotherhood of Stargazers, or whatever it was.

"My reply was, she had no proof that Aunt had sent me money to invest. Her reply to that was that the document to prove it, the original, drawn up and signed by Aunt, was in Los Angeles. That if I'd meet her views she'd send for it and turn it over to me. If she turned it over to the authorities, it would finish me.

"As you may imagine, I was flustered. We stood there in the road, and it wasn't even dark; late twilight, June thirtieth. Poor Aunt's body collapsed in the car, and the Drummonds might drive by any minute. Not likely this summer, but they used their station wagon too, for necessary trips. Perhaps *they* were having guests!

"I made my mistake. I asked Gouch what she proposed."

Blanche Drummond cried out: "But what else could you have done, Johnny?"

"I could have killed her, Blanche." He turned a sadly smiling face in her direction. "But Gamadge reminded you that I'm not a habitual criminal. I'm civilized.

"Well, of course, you all know now what she had in mind; an inspiration born of circumstance. For the station had been crowded, and she'd heard me say that I didn't know our porter, and here was my place to dispose of a body in. We'd just passed the gate that leads in to the swimming pool, and I'd mentioned the fact.

"A truly sublime idea of Gouch's, and one that gives you the full measure of her greed. She wanted the seven thousand that was in the bank, of course; but the Stargazers' cut bothered her. She felt quite robbed by it. She insisted on having a try at the July income installment too. Not that she had much to lose if the check with the forged indorsement didn't go through—she had only to disappear. I was the one who'd be ruined. But I may say now that it did go through, and so did the October one—she was so elated by our initial success that she extended her tour, stayed on. Why shouldn't my forgery have succeeded? I knew Aunt's signature well enough, and had specimens of it; and I'm supposed to be an artist"—he smiled grimly—"in black and white.

"But perhaps you can imagine the tortures I went through all summer. I wasn't much afraid of old residents who had known her in her youth turning up, and I could be mighty careful not to let them see her if they should turn up; but there's always the possibility of accident."

Gamadge asked: "That party you gave for her on the tenth of July was her first public appearance, wasn't it?"

"Yes."

"You told us last night that her income payments came in July and October. I wondered whether you had waited for the check to get back to Los Angeles and go through the bank before you finally risked the party."

"You wondered *then?*"

"I already suspected an impersonation, Johnny."

"Yes. Of course. And she waited for the second check to go through before leaving; she meant to go this week.

"Her future plans for acquiring Aunt's money were to my mind risky and uncertain to the last degree; but what could I do? I only hoped that they would succeed. They wouldn't leave her worse off if they failed, I was the one they'd destroy in that case. Her idea was to build up a reputation here for eccentricity—the sun cult took care of that—and then disappear. Evidence would point to accidental death or suicide. She might have pulled it off; she was clever, much cleverer than you would have guessed from her behavior in her role of eccentric, and she had every reason for pulling it off. If she didn't, she wouldn't get Aunt's estate for years, if ever. Aunt would have to be presumed dead.

"Well, sketchy as her plan was, I had to fall in with it; and as I intimated before, I was pretty sure nobody at Rivertown Station had noticed that I had two women with me instead of one—nobody but a strange porter who was trying to serve a dozen other people besides us. I had the key of the gate on me—I always do. We carried poor Aunt's body into the grounds, and then got her luggage. Gouch unpacked her own bags in the car. She unpacked Aunt's things, all but the garments and stuff you specified, and filled up with hers. She worked it all out on the spot—about the shoes and so on; and it seems that she'd always had a covetous eye on those house robes, or tea gowns, or whatever they were.

"I thought of the old watering trough. It may sound pretty ghastly to you people, but it was a gift of the gods to me that evening. I got the lid off somehow—you don't want those details. Gamadge has told you what's there.

"Next morning I was down early and piled the undergrowth, and tried to think of something to prop up. I thought of the wooden image in the garage.

"She was delighted with it, and from the moment she saw it the sun cult was born. She enjoyed it all; she enjoyed meeting the children and acting the part of benefactress which poor Aunt had always wanted to act herself. She didn't care, of course, whether they liked her or not; but she couldn't resist getting back at them when she saw they couldn't stand her. That's why she handed Cora that pin, with Cora's mother's diamonds pinned on the front of the yellow thing she sported. Handed Cora the pin, and gave herself away.

"You can imagine whether I hated her. You can imagine whether I trusted her to send me that signed statement, and how much I liked the idea of waiting for it until I had sent her my share of the thirty thousand. But it wasn't until the very moment when I came in here and saw the rifle . . .

"I was in the vegetable garden, you know; I saw Cora go up through the woods, as I thought to the house. I saw Blanche cross to the greenhouse, and David go down the Loop. I knew where Abby was. I thought Drummond was busy in the flower garden, cutting me something or other—and so he was. I needed that weeder, and I needed the extra basket. I went across and cut into this place from the east. I heard your voice, Gamadge, and hers, as you went up to the rockery. I spied through those vines in that corner—I wondered how much of a fool she might be making of herself with you. I saw her against that birch tree.

"And I turned, and there was the rifle in that thing's arms. He seemed—I swear he seemed to be offering it to me. I wondered if it were loaded. Gamadge, I saw all my troubles falling away; there had been crow shooting, it might be considered an accident, and in any case there were so many of us to choose from that I thought we'd all be safe. I can't work things out as you do. I knew I'd never be suspected, nobody'd ever bother Los Angeles, and I thought I'd offer my financial motive as a cover for the children. I'm not hard up, credit's good, they could check if they liked.

"I stood there and looked at the rifle, and I thought: I'll leave it to the gods. If it's loaded, I'm meant to be free. If it isn't, I'm meant to pay for that five thousand a year I spent on myself. But I thought it was loaded, because the gods had given me those gloves and that spud.

"I loosened the turf and piled it, no use letting them *know* the rifle had been fired by a tall woman or a shortish man. I got the rifle, and I sighted through the vines. And there she still was, the horror of a woman, with her arms spread out, looking at me! Only she didn't know it."

Redfield made that helpless gesture with both hands. He said: "I've killed a hundred crows."

"Well," he resumed, "I got out of there, and the

moment I was out I was safe; I had only to turn and
be coming back through the wicket. And that's all of
that. Oh—one thing more. For a long time—I had all
summer I thought about that signed document. The
more I thought about it, the surer I was that she had
it with her; she wouldn't let me put my nose into her
room, even to bring flowers, and she kept it locked
when I wasn't under her eye. After the medical examiner finished with her they let me go up and put
away the jewelry—why not? I hung up the yellow
robe with a couple of the country men right there
with me, and I felt the paper in the hem. I had it out
and in my pocket in twenty seconds. You missed those
few loose stitches, Gamadge."

"I hadn't the data to imagine a document, Johnny,
and I wasn't looking for one. I was checking on the
clothes and shoes. I did go through the pockets,
hoping for a sign of Gouch's identity, but I didn't
find one."

"But when I found that document I thought I was
safe. And then—" all Redfield's sang froid fell away.
He looked wildly about him. "Then that other
woman came. I'd never seen her, I never dreamed
she'd gone out to Pasadena and seen Aunt Josephine.
Aunt didn't mention it, and I'm sure Gouch didn't
know. She'd never have risked the game if she had
known. I suppose the woman was there after my visit,
and Aunt decided not to put it in a letter."

"It was obvious you'd never met her," said Gamadge.

"The moment Blanche left us, after we went upstairs, she sprung it on me. Blackmail again, and just
when I'd gone through—no. I couldn't stand it. We
had just come into the bedroom, and I stopped to see

if the reading light was working. It didn't seem to go on; I took off the shade to unscrew the bulb. She walked back past me and shut the door, and she stood there and came right out with it; 'Mr. Redfield, I dropped in on Mrs. Archibald Malcolm last spring in Pasadena.' Just like that, and by the grin on her face I knew what the game was going to be.

"After what I'd been through it was too much. My brain gave. She strutted past me, never thought of the lamp. A lamp's a lamp, bedside ones usually have short cords; but this one had a long cord—there used to be twin beds, with the night table between.

"And I'm such a harmless-looking little man. But I snatched up the bedspread and held it in front of me, and I snatched up the lamp, and I—" He made a furious gesture with his clenched hand.

"There wasn't a spot on my fingers." He lifted his hands, looked at them, and let them fall at his sides. "There wasn't a spot on me anywhere. But I went to my room and washed, and afterwards I came down to the studio and talked to Griggs. I felt quite calm. I didn't think she'd be found until morning. You weren't any more startled than I was, Gamadge, either of you, when Blanche screamed. And I never thought until afterwards what it would mean to David Malcolm."

Gamadge stood looking down at him. Then, when he said no more, but sat as if exhausted by the memory of what he had described for them, Gamadge turned to the others. "Ladies and gentlemen of the jury," he said, "the defense evidently rests."

19

Verdict

Drummond slowly and deliberately lighted his pipe, got it going well, and then spoke: "Don't know what we're supposed to do about it. Even if we all decided to let him run for it, how is he to get away, and where would he go, and what would happen to us afterwards? What would happen to you?"

"I have some ideas on the subject," replied Gamadge. "The police don't suspect Redfield; he could walk out of this place and up to the house without being stopped or questioned. He could see Griggs, and tell him the conference hadn't come to anything—I'm afraid Griggs wouldn't be surprised to hear it—and ask if he might drive down to Old Bridge for supplies. Griggs would understand the necessity. He'd find out that we were still safely boxed up in here, and I think he'd let Johnny go.

"I was careful to set the conference early, and the inquest doesn't come off until two o'clock. Johnny could drive to Old Bridge and draw his balance out of the bank. He has a good balance there—he gave us that impression yesterday. If he said he needed plenty of cash for expenses connected with his aunt's funeral, and all the rest of it—no; they'd ask no questions at Old Bridge.

"And they'd ask none at his bank in New York. He could be in New York, drawing his balance there, before he was even missed at Idlers. Shopping takes a long time in these days, I dare say Redfield shops all over the country for one thing or another. Griggs would understand that.

"Redfield could get rid of his car, take a bus or train, and lose himself."

"Yes," said Drummond dryly, "he could. And we'd all go to jail as accessories after the fact to a double murder."

"Oh, no; nothing would happen to us at all. When he didn't appear for the inquest we'd all show horror and surprise—it needn't be hard for us, it's pretty much what we feel now—and then I'd get busy thinking. I'd think of Gouch again, Griggs knows I was interested in her from the start. I'd explain that I never had been able to understand why she stayed on doing all that work for Mrs. Malcolm after she was under dismissal and in disgrace. That was a weak point in Redfield's story, and I should simply imply that it hadn't struck me forcibly until now.

"Then I'd insist on a call to Los Angeles and one to Pasadena, and Griggs would have a description of both women. Then I'd begin to construct the theory that you all heard just now. I'd trot out the Regard pin—Griggs would suppose that it had been in Miss Malcolm's possession ever since the impostor gave it to her—and I'd bring up the matter of the tea gowns that weren't long enough, and the sandals that would stay on larger feet than they were bought for, and the sun cult, and everything else. I'd remember that there was a watering trough; but perhaps when I called Griggs' attention to the propped statue, and the loose underbrush behind it I wouldn't have to say anything about the watering trough at all.

"Griggs would have the whole case against Redfield, motive would probably build up later, and we'd all leave the inquest without a stain on our characters."

Blanche asked anxiously: "Yes, but where would Johnny *go?*"

Cora Malcolm was looking down at her brother; remorse was on her face, but a great relief too. She said: "Mightn't he stay at our apartment until he made some plans? It's a walk-up; and nobody'd think of looking for him there."

"No," said Gamadge, smiling at her. "Nobody'd think of looking for him there. Am I to understand that you are all ready to face these risks—for in all illegal operations there must be risk—and let Redfield go?" He looked from one to another of them. "Is that the verdict of you all? Extenuating circumstances and recommendation to mercy?"

Blanche said: "Poor Johnny; poor Johnny. Let him go."

"You realize that if he killed twice when cornered he might kill again? That your life mightn't have been worth much, Blanche, if you'd happened to face him alone in this place, with my theory, and he'd been armed? *I* shouldn't have risked it!"

"He was driven to killing those women. He was desperate."

"It might have been your earring that he dropped here, instead of Miss Malcolm's pin."

"It wasn't, though. We don't know what he'd have done if it had been my earring."

"You feel no resentment towards him on account of his attack on your character?"

"My character? What do you mean?"

"His comments on your feeling about money."

"Johnny understands. He only talked like that because he was desperate. When people are desperate they say things they don't mean at all. It wasn't as bad as thinking I'd committed the murders!"

"Well: your reasons for clemency are personal, Blanche. But we must accept them. Miss Malcolm, you have already implied that you would like Redfield to escape."

"Yes. I should."

"No remark of mine is required here. Mr. Malcolm?"

"Cora remembers, as I do, that Mr. Redfield was kind to us and that my mother liked him."

"As devil's advocate I ought to remind you that his interest in you all may not have been altruistic. Some day you would be very well off. He may have thought that day would come soon; your father's second marriage adjourned it."

"I don't think that friendliness such as Mr. Redfield showed us all in Switzerland can be assumed. I think he is normally considerate and kind."

"He was leaving you and perhaps your sister to the gods."

"I must echo Mrs. Drummond: we don't know what he would have done in the end."

"You think we should be dealing fairly with society in letting him go?"

"Yes; I do. But even if I didn't, I couldn't personally hand him over to the police."

"Thanks. Drummond?"

Drummond took his pipe out of his mouth. "For God's sake get him started."

Gamadge turned and looked down at Redfield. "I must say, Johnny, that your friends are behaving towards you, in a manner that if not technically civilized is certainly humane."

Redfield managed to smile. "They are indeed. But"—he got slowly to his feet—"I don't think I shall take advantage of their magnanimity, or of yours." He slightly lifted his shoulders, and dropped them. "I don't see the future. Too much suspense, too little relaxation, too little ease for a quiet man of my age. But thank you all very much."

He walked to the archway without another glance at anyone, and through it. They heard his voice raised outside: "Hi, Officer. What's-your-name—in the rockery, there . . . Come and get me. I'm giving myself up."

Gamadge said, looking after him, "I knew he would."

Drummond got up and gestured with a clenched hand. "I'd have shot myself. Gone off somewhere and bought a gun and shot myself."

"Redfield could never do that."

Blanche Drummond burst out crying, and left the rose garden. Drummond groaned: "I have no right to follow her."

"She'll go to Abby, Walter."

Malcolm, his head lowered and all his spirit in eclipse, slowly pulled up blades of grass. Cora said, her eyes turned from them all: "It will take a long time for us to get over this. A long time."

20

Man with a Headache

Miss Abigail Ryder's living room was a pleasant place on an October afternoon at tea time. Apple wood, living up to its reputation, sang in the white fireplace. Firelight shone on old brasses and copper, and on the gilt of gold mirrors. Purple and white asters in the copper pots matched the fading chintzes and window curtains.

It was the twelfth, a holiday, and Gamadge had stayed over. He sat opposite his cousin and drank tea from a mauve-and-gilt cup.

"Blanche called me from New York this morning," said Abby.

"She'll be better off there. She'll find somebody," said Gamadge.

"Henry, you are so vulgar."

"Do *you* think she won't?"

"No matter how badly she may have behaved, I shouldn't blame her if she never did forgive Walter for thinking she committed the murders."

"She was very much wrought up, Abby. She wasn't herself at all. She was behaving so madly that I can excuse Drummond for thinking she'd gone quite off her base."

"That Malcolm boy behaved shockingly. Shockingly at first in having the affair with her at all, and then shockingly to her."

"He was shocked himself at the way she was reacting. He was rather young to have a grand passion on his hands. I'm very glad," said Gamadge, passing his cup for more tea, "that Drummond can presently pursue his beautiful friendship with Miss Malcolm."

Miss Ryder said crossly, putting less sugar into his cup than he liked, "I keep telling you that it was a friendship. They were friends long before the brother almost broke it up by entering into this wretched affair with Blanche."

"I know it was a friendship," said Gamadge, taking his cup from her and helping himself to a lump from the sugar bowl. "The most beautiful kind. They love each other. I suppose they had a pretty tragic time of it down there in the garden on Sunday afternoon behind the cosmos. She'd be saying that she and her brother must never come up here again, and he'd be begging her to let him try to work out a divorce with Blanche, scrape up enough money to give Blanche enough alimony to suit her. And she'd reply that while Blanche felt as she did about Malcolm the whole thing was too ugly, a horrid quadrangle. Then she left him forever, and went up to grieve in the tool house. No wonder he didn't see people going or coming from the orchard, no wonder it took time for her to remember that game of croquet. But when I nab my favorite mallet I nab the ball too. Well, they'll be all right now. Where are the Malcolms, by the way?"

"They're at that inn at Old Bridge where you never get anything to eat but creamed canned chicken and make-believe fruit jelly."

Gamadge craned forward in his chair as steps sounded on the porch. "*He* isn't."

"Is that David Malcolm coming?"

"Yes."

Miss Ryder's local help ushered David Malcolm into the living room. He begged pardon for arriving at teatime, was made politely welcome by his hostess, accepted tea, and sat down opposite the fire. He looked subdued, handsome, and thoughtful.

"I don't think I'll ever get over it," he said. "I feel very low about it. I never even guessed at Redfield."

Gamadge, eating a crumpet, said that they knew whom he'd guessed at.

"And wasn't that brutal of me? But don't let's go into the matter of brutalities, or I shall get a headache. Mr. Gamadge, could you suggest a job for a man with occasional headaches?"

"Yes."

"You *could?*"

"Assistant to me. Mine's left me—going to set up as an analytical chemist after the war, if he gets through it. But you couldn't live in, you know," said Gamadge, passing the crumpets. "My assistant lived on the top floor; now that's going to be given over to a young infant with his nurse, the electric stove and refrigerator out of my laboratory—till the war's over and I can get others—and about ten thousand bottles."

Malcolm gazed at him.

"But you'd have the run of the inferior floors," continued Gamadge, "and two big libraries—one in the office, one upstairs. You could almost learn the trade from them. And"—Gamadge smiled—"you could almost learn to write from them. Even a perfectionist could."

"You mean this, Mr. Gamadge?"

"Certainly I mean it. As for the occasional headaches, I should ask you to consult a friend of mine named Hamish. You couldn't have afforded him before, his charges are awful, but I'll tell him you're going to have plenty of money, and he'll put off sending a bill."

Malcolm sat with his untasted tea in its lustre cup balanced on his hand. He asked: "Would you mind telling me, Mr. Gamadge, why you're offering me this?"

"Of course I'll tell you. I never in my life saw anybody stand up to anything as you stood up to the danger you thought you were confronted with on Sunday."

There was a silence. Then Malcolm, glancing at Abigail Ryder, said; "I'd been rather asking for something. My general attitude and conduct had been—er—irresponsible. It all seemed to have resulted in trouble for Cora as well as for myself, and I thought the only sensible thing would be to keep my wits and face the thing seriously.

"Let me have such men about me," murmured Gamadge, "fat or thin."

Abby said: "Mr. Malcolm, you must try these cakes."

Malcolm took one. "Thanks, Miss Ryder. I ought to say that Cora and I had some experience in keeping our wits in France. We managed to get some British out before we left. That's why we were a little worried about our own getaway—we were earmarked. Wouldn't you think"—he looked from Abigail to Gamadge—"that I could have managed to put up with *anything* from that unfortunate wife of mine?"

Miss Ryder said: "I don't see the obligation. You hadn't bargained for blackmail."

"To tell you the truth, Miss Ryder—there's no use in being hypocritical about it—at one time I didn't much care what she might be capable of. But you wouldn't know about that."

Miss Ryder changed the subject: "Are you staying on with your sister in your flat?"

"If you'll excuse me for referring to such a delicate matter, she won't be with me so very long. Do you realize that I almost ruined *that* for her?"

"Well, really!" She looked at him over the tops of her steel spectacles. "Walter Drummond was married, you know!"

"The stars attended to that," smiled Malcolm, and then he frowned at himself. "Lord, that nightmare! Can I be joking about it?"

"I shall never joke about it," said Abigail, "and nobody feels worse about it than I do; but I don't intend to let it ruin my life."

"You adopt my cousin's attitude towards it," said Gamadge, "and you won't go wrong. It's settled then—your job with me. I shall be in my house permanently by the first of November."

"I wish to heaven you'd ask me to do something difficult, instead of doing me a favor. Great heavens, won't you *take* that ten thousand dollars?"

"No," said Gamadge. "I can't say that I was fond of Redfield, but I liked him."

ELIZABETH DALY burst upon the American
mystery scene at the outbreak of World War II.
Her straightforward detective, Gamadge, has
received high praise from writers and critics.
DEATH AND LETTERS, first published in 1950,
is considered a classic and is also a selection of
the Dell MURDER INK.® Mystery Series.

MURDER INK.® is the renowned mystery book-
store in New York City. The small shop, with
books stacked from floor to ceiling, special-
izes in popular mysteries and collectors' clas-
sics. ANY SHAPE OR FORM has been selected
by Ms. Carol Brener, proprietor of Murder Ink.
and editorial consultant for the Dell MURDER
INK. Mystery Series.

ANY SHAPE OR FORM

Johnny Redfield's aunt came from California, insisted on using her "astral" name, and claimed to belong to a mysterious cult. At the cocktail party in her honor, the wealthy, eccentric widow had served up nothing but insults all afternoon.

Now she lay with a bullet in her head in Johnny's English rose garden. Every guest had good reason to wish her dead. But only the ingenious Henry Gamadge could weed out the clue that pointed to a desperate killer with nothing left to lose by striking again.

PRINTED IN USA

10108

0

71009 00225

ISBN 0-440-10108-5